The author is a semi-retired teacher who lives in the English Midlands. Visits to old mine workings in North Wales, one of which has an underground lake, together with his Welsh ancestry provided part of the inspiration for this book.

This book is dedicated to my grandsons, Alex and Daniel, without whom it would not have been written.

William Roberts

THOMAS AND CAITLIN:

BOOK ONE:

THE CAVES OF CAERDRAIG

AUSTIN MACAULEY
PUBLISHERS LTD.

A CIP catalogue record for this title is available from the British Library.

ISBN 9781786127372 (Paperback)
ISBN 9781786127389 (Hardback)
ISBN 9781786127396 (EBook)

www.austinmacauley.com

First Published (2016)
Austin Macauley Publishers Ltd.
25 Canada Square
Canary Wharf
London
E14 5LQ

Chapter 1

Thomas and Caitlin

Evan stirred. Half-awake he thought he could hear something... or was he dreaming? He raised his head from the pillow and listened. No, the noises were real: strange grunts and growls mixed with the bleats of lambs and barks of dogs. Slipping quietly out of bed, he went over to the window and eased the shutter open. In the yard below, something huge slowly moved along in the shadow cast by the cottage. Emerging into the moonlight, it ignored the dogs snapping at its feet, crossed the yard and disappeared behind the bushes fronting the pen where the lambs were kept.

Evan did not hesitate. He pulled on his boots and with his wife Gwyn following, quickly descended the ladder from the loft where they slept. Reaching the outside door, he stopped. Trembling with fear he lifted the heavy wooden bar that secured it and eased it open, just enough to see through. A giant lizard-like creature emerged from behind the bushes with one of his lambs wrapped in its long thin tail. It really was enormous, many times the size of his cow, and in the moonlight looked black. Evan swallowed hard and edged forward.

"Evan, come back. It'll kill you!" Gwyn shouted, grasping his arm tightly.

Evan ignored her. Pulling his arm away he went outside.

The monster spotted him, swung its head in his direction, blinked its yellow slit eyes and growled, a low rumbling growl. Lowering its head, it opened its mouth to expose an awesome set of long pointed teeth, and hissed. Evan backed away. Grabbing a pitchfork leaning against the cottage wall, he held it out in front of him. The monster roared, raised its front leg and swept him off his feet, leaving him sprawling in the mud. Turning rapidly, it made off towards the nearby forest, the piteously bleating lamb still wrapped in its tail. Without thinking of the danger Evan ran after it, but it was too fast for him. Soon he lost sight of it among the trees.

With thundering hearts and white faces, Evan and Gwyn went back inside. For some time, they were too shocked to speak.

Eventually Gwyn spoke. "I hope the children aren't awake. If they've seen the monster they'll have nightmares." She went up the ladder, had a look and came down.

"All are fast asleep, thank the Lord. We mustn't tell them about it, but we must insist they don't go near the forest anymore."

Evan was thinking about his animals. "Just think, whenever I found an animal missing I blamed passing tramps or outlaws. How wrong I was."

Gwyn was worried. "What are we to do, Evan? How can we tackle such a huge beast? It might come back again and again, until we have no animals left."

"All we can do is make sure all the animals are locked up before the sun sets," he said.

Thomas and Caitlin were Evan and Gwyn's two oldest children. Caitlin was ten years old and Thomas a year older. Like their parents they had brown eyes and brown hair, Caitlin's being lighter and longer than her brother's. On a winter's night, tucked up warm in their sheepskin covered beds, they would listen to the rushing sound the wind made in the forest trees, a comforting sound which lulled them to sleep, but often there were other sounds. Some they knew well, such as the snarling barks of foxes and the screeches and hoots of owls, but they sometimes heard deep growls and roaring noises that made their blood run cold. Frightened, they hid under the sheepskins until eventually sleep overcame them. Those sounds and the thought of what might have uttered them, made them wary of going deep into the forest so they always stayed near its edge.

Next morning Thomas and Caitlin came crashing down the ladder ready for breakfast. The stern expression on their father's face told them something was wrong.

"Listen!" he said. "You often play in the forest, don't you?"

"Yes."

"And you always play near its edge, like I told you?"

"Yes."

"Good ... but now you are not to go anywhere near it."

"Why?" they both cried in surprise.

"I've heard that some children in the next village have been attacked by wolves."

"Is it true?" asked Thomas. "We've been there lots of times and never seen a wolf."

"Don't question me. Just do as you're told!" Evan sounded cross.

"Alright," they both said sulkily.

Evan wondered whether he was the only farmer in the district who was having animals taken, and decided to find out. The following evening, he went to the village inn where he met some of his neighbours. He told them about the monster stealing a lamb. Some of the farmers didn't believe him. They laughed.

"Good try, Evan," said Iolo, "but I'm not fooled."

"I've told you the truth. I'm not trying to fool anyone!" said Evan sharply.

The farmers murmured among themselves until Robert said, "Well, now I've heard your story, I'll tell you mine. I've never told anybody before because I didn't think they'd believe me."

"One morning last autumn I was woken at dawn by pigs squealing, geese cackling and dogs barking. I thought a fox was trying to catch my hens, so I quickly pulled on some clothes, picked up the stick I keep next to my bed, and rushed outside. I almost bumped into an enormous creature standing just outside my door, so big its back was almost level with the eaves of the cottage roof."

Evan interrupted him. "The one I saw was big, but not as big as that."

Iolo said, "Perhaps there's more than one of them."

Robert continued. "Well, it was very big ... and ugly, and had wings like a bat. Dangling from its mouth was a dead pig. I shouted and waved my stick, hoping to make it drop the pig, but as soon as it saw me, it beat its wings and flew off taking the pig with it."

"That's odd," said Evan, "I'm sure mine didn't have wings."

He felt uneasy. Making for the door he said "I must hurry back in case the beast returns."

"Aye, me too," said Iolo.

One by one the farmers slipped away, worried about their animals.

The track Evan took home skirted the forest. Tall trees, with bushes and brambles growing beneath, edged the path. In the rapidly fading light, the forest looked dark and threatening. Every little noise made him jump. His heart skipped a beat and raced. Many times he imagined he saw the monster's dark shape lurking in the bushes. He hurried on, constantly glancing back to make sure nothing was following. At last the end of the path came into view. He began to relax. With one last look behind, he quickly crossed the fields to his cottage.

Back home, Evan checked that all his animals were securely locked up and went indoors. That night he hardly slept. Each sound made him jump out of bed and rush to the window. However, the night passed without incident and so did the rest of the week.

The whole family worked hard. Although they always had enough to eat, they didn't have much money for anything else. One reason was the theft of animals. Another was the need to pay rent to the Earl who lived in the castle on the hill near the village. This castle was called Caerdraig (Castle of the Dragon), because there was a huge statue of a dragon just outside its main gates.

One hot summer's night Thomas and Caitlin were finding it difficult to sleep. After a while Caitlin got up.

"Thomas, I'm thirsty. I'm going down to get some water. D'you want some?"

As she approached the top of the ladder, she heard her mother talking.

"Evan, all our clothes are very ragged and the children's clothes have holes in them. I'll have to make new ones. When we go to the Midsummer Fair next month, we must buy some cloth."

Evan frowned. "I'm afraid we don't have much money, Gwyn, not enough to buy cloth for us all."

"Well the children must come first. You and I will have to wait until next year."

Aware that Caitlin was descending the ladder they stopped talking. Caitlin said nothing, drank a cup of water and returned to the bedroom, taking some for Thomas.

She told him what she had heard. "I wish we could find some money. It doesn't seem fair for us to have new clothes while Mum and Dad go without."

They lay in bed wondering what they might do until Thomas had an idea.

"You know that cave in the cliff near the river?"

"Yes?" replied Caitlin, wondering what it had to do with money.

"Well, it's said to lead to some old Roman silver mines. Perhaps there's still some silver left. We could go and look."

Caitlin didn't like the idea. "Mum and Dad have told us never to go in there because it's dangerous."

Thomas persisted. "We won't go far inside and if it looks dangerous, we'll come straight out."

"No Thomas! We must do as Mum and Dad tell us. They know best."

"But we'll be quite safe. We'll only go a little way inside."

"Thomas, no!"

Thomas knew it was useless to argue and said nothing more.

Chapter 2

The Afon Glas

Morning came. Thomas and Caitlin washed their hands and faces in a bowl of warm water, ate some porridge and drank a cup of water.

While eating, Thomas said "Caitlin, d'you want to come down to the river after breakfast?"

"Yes. Perhaps some of our friends will be there."

Their mother heard what they were planning to do. "That's alright, but before you go, make sure you've done all your jobs."

"What do we have to do today?" asked Caitlin.

"Caitlin, you let the hens, ducks and geese out of the shed and give them some corn, and Thomas, bring me two buckets of water from the well. Then go to the cowshed and help your father milk the cow."

They had little work to do that day but quite often had more. Caitlin would help her mother chop wood for the fire, wash clothes in the river, make bread, butter or cheese and mind the baby. Meanwhile, Thomas would help his father with whatever work needed to be done. This depended on the season. It might be cleaning manure out of the cowshed, digging ditches, ploughing the land with the ox, guarding the sheep or weeding vegetable plots. The amount of work was greatest in spring and autumn and least in winter. However, midsummer was also a quiet time and, with little work to do, Thomas and Caitlin had time to play and explore the surrounding countryside.

Like most children over a thousand years ago, Thomas and Caitlin didn't go to school.

To be educated, children had to be sent away to an abbey to be taught by a monk or a nun, and few people could afford to pay for that.

A short distance from the cottage was a river called the Afon Glas. Upstream from the cottage it emerged from a tunnel in the side of a low hill and flowed down past the cottage to the village. Part way, it passed the cave that was said to be the entrance to the old silver mines. On the other side of the river rose a low clay cliff, on top of which grew the forest. In winter, the river was a raging torrent of blue-green water, but in summer it was a broad shallow pebbly stream, so shallow you could walk across it without the water even coming over the tops of your boots. Where the river went they did not know, until their father told them that after it left their valley, it joined a bigger river which after many miles flowed into the sea. Thomas and Caitlin knew the Afon Glas and the near part of the forest well, often spending the long days of summer playing there with their friends.

When they arrived at the river that morning, none of their friends were there so they had to amuse themselves. First they paddled in the river and caught a couple of little fish. Having looked at them closely, they let them go. Then they went to the place where the river flowed out from under the hill. Here it formed a pool of deep water.

"Let's go for a swim," said Thomas.

They took off their clothes, dived in and swam up and down the pool a few times.

"Caitlin, I'm going to find out where the river comes from." said Thomas.

"Huh! You won't succeed. We've all tried to do it lots of times, and nobody has ever managed it."

"Well, this time I will!"

He swam underwater towards where the river emerged from under the hill, but the nearer he got the swifter the current became and he did not have the strength to overcome it. Swept back to where he started from, he tried a second time ... and again he failed.

Caitlin laughed and said, "I told you so."

Thomas was irritated. He splashed her with lots of water, but she laughed even more.

"Caitlin, I've had enough of swimming. Have you?"

"Yes."

"Let's go and play on the swing."

Caitlin stared at him. "That's among the trees on the edge of the forest. Dad's told us not to go there."

"It's only on the edge. We've been there lots of times and not come to any harm. Why should it be different now?"

She couldn't think of a reason. "I don't know... well... alright, I suppose we'll be safe."

Just as they were leaving the water, something in the mud at the water's edge caught Thomas's eye.

"Look at those footprints. They're enormous!"

They squatted down to examine them.

"Wow!" said Caitlin. "None of the animals in the forest have feet as big as those." They stared at the footprints.

"Thomas, do you think what the villagers say about monsters living in the forest is true?"

"No, I don't!" he snapped. "If such monsters existed we would've seen them."

"Not if they only come out at night," said Caitlin.

Thomas didn't want to believe monsters lived in the forest: the thought frightened him.

"I think the footprints were made by a big bear. I hope it's not still around," he said.

Caitlin looked at the footprints again and remarked "If there are monsters, they must be very big and very fierce. I hope we don't meet them."

They both looked around nervously and listened intently, but could neither see nor hear anything unusual. After a while they decided they were safe and got dressed.

Crossing the river, they walked along the edge of the forest. Soon they came to the swing. Dangling from a branch of a big oak tree was a rope. This had been tied to the branch by their friend Huw who had been brave enough to climb the tree. The bottom of the rope was tied to the middle of a short stout stick. Caitlin sat on the stick and held onto the rope. Thomas took hold of the ends of the stick, pulled it back and let go. Caitlin started to swing backwards and forwards. Each time she swung back, Thomas pushed her gently.

"Higher," she commanded. Thomas pushed harder.

"Higher!"

He pushed harder still. Now she went so high she began to feel unsafe and was frightened she might fall off.

She let out a little scream and shouted, "Not this high!"

He pushed her again and laughed as she screamed once more.

Suddenly she stopped screaming and shouted, "Quick, let me down!"

Her request sounded urgent so Thomas let the swing slow down and stop.

He looked at her pale frightened face and said, "I'm sorry. I didn't mean to upset you."

"I thought I saw something," she said.

"What?"

"I thought I saw the head of a huge green animal among the trees."

"You're imagining things."

"No I'm not," she said indignantly.

Cautiously, they walked towards the trees where Caitlin thought she had seen the animal. They stood and stared but couldn't see anything.

"I think you must have imagined it," said Thomas scornfully.

"I don't think so," she said, but she didn't sound too sure.

In silence they walked back to the swing.

After a while she said, "Well ... I'm not absolutely certain. It could just have been a shape made by the branches and the leaves."

Leaving the swing, they set off to find the den they had made a few weeks earlier. They often made dens out of fallen branches, twigs and leaves, so that when it rained they had somewhere to shelter. The wind had blown leaves and twigs off it and the sky could be seen through its roof. Before they left, they repaired the damage.

The forest had many mysteries. In some parts there was dense undergrowth, with great tangles of brambles and thorn bushes, which often made it impossible to continue on one's way, whilst in other parts there was only a sparse covering of grass. In the grassy areas, many of the tall trees had some of their higher branches broken off ... as if something big and tall had brushed against them. Some of these damaged trees, and parts of the ground around them, were scorched even though there was no sign of a forest fire. Also, here and there in the forest, enormous mounds of earth mixed with clay and stones, kept appearing.

A short distance from their shelter, they spied a fresh mound.

"That mound wasn't there when we were last here," said Thomas.

"No, it wasn't," agreed Caitlin. "I wonder where it's come from."

"Some people in the village say the mounds are made by moles as big as sheep, but others say giants living in the hills come during the night and dump the earth in the forest."

"Why should they do that?"

"I don't know. Nobody has ever said why they do it." Both were puzzled.

Another forest mystery was the existence of several large deep pits, dug so long ago that grass and bushes now grew in them. Who had dug them, and for what purpose, nobody knew. In one of these pits, half-hidden among the grass and bushes, were the mouldering bones of some kind of huge animal. From their poor condition, it was evident they must have lain there for a very long time.

Thomas was in an adventurous mood. "Let's go and look at the bones in the pit."

Caitlin was a bit nervous about going to the pit because it wasn't close to the edge of the forest. "I don't think we should go there. It mightn't be safe. Dad told us some children have been attacked by wolves."

"I don't believe it. We've never ever seen a wolf in the forest," asserted Thomas.

"That's true, but I'm still not sure," she said.

24

"But we've been there before and it's been safe."

She considered the matter and said, "Well ... I suppose you're right. Let's go."

They made their way through the trees to the pit and looked down at the bones.

"What has bones as big as those?" asked Thomas.

"None of the animals we know," said Caitlin.

Then, with a note of alarm in her voice, she said, "Perhaps they're from one of the monsters that live in this forest!"

"There aren't any monsters!" shouted Thomas.

Thomas was fed up with hearing about monsters, whose possible existence secretly terrified him. "Anyway, we can't decide what sort of animal left those bones until we've had a close look at them. Let's go down and look."

Slowly and carefully they made their way down to the bottom of the pit. The bones, their surfaces pitted with age, had been bleached by the sun and were partly covered in moss. They examined the animal's skull. It was much bigger than it looked when seen from the top of the pit and was about the size of a fully grown pig. Thomas crawled beneath it and put his head through one of the eye sockets.

"It's much too big to be a bear's skull, isn't it?" asserted Caitlin.

"I suppose it is," admitted Thomas rather reluctantly.

Behind the skull were lots of other bones including huge ribs, thick heavy leg bones, an enormous pelvic bone, long thin arm bones (from which hung leathery tatters) and a long line of vertebrae. Clearly, this animal must have had a bulky body, large wings and a long tail.

The pointed teeth and sharp claws caught Thomas's attention.

"Whatever it was, I wouldn't have liked to have met it. Look at those claws and teeth! It would have killed and eaten us."

Caitlin shuddered at the thought of it.

Having had a good look at the bones, they started to clamber up the side of the pit. Halfway up, they heard growling noises coming from a bush at the top. Something was hiding in it.

"Oh no!" exclaimed Caitlin in a worried voice, "a bear has spotted us."

"Quick, let's go before it gets us!"

They scrambled out of the pit and ran towards the river, but stopped when they heard raucous laughter. Out of the bush sprang Huw.

"Huw! You scared us. Just wait till I get you," shouted Thomas.

Huw took one look at their cross faces and ran off. They chased after him until all were quite out of breath. Having caught up with Huw, Thomas ruffled his hair. Huw just laughed. All three then walked through the trees towards the path that ran alongside the river.

Chapter 3

Emrys

Reaching the path, they plodded along in single file for some minutes. Soon they began to feel bored and wondered what to do next.

Thomas said, "Let's go to the village and ask Emrys to tell us a story."

"Good idea!" said Caitlin.

However, Huw said he could not go with them because he had to go home to feed the pigs, and off he went.

Shortly a tall, slim and pretty young woman, wearing a black cloak over a long red dress, came hurrying along the path. As she passed by, she smiled at them.

"Thomas, I haven't seen her round here before," whispered Caitlin. "Have you?"

"No, I wonder who she is?"

In the whole district there were only two people who could read and write. One was the priest and the other was Emrys. People depended on them for writing letters and also for some entertainment. The priest read villagers stories from his Bible, stories that carried a message and made them think, while Emrys told anyone who cared to listen all sorts of fantastic stories. Some of these he had memorised but others he read from one of his scrolls.

Emrys lived in a tiny tumbledown cottage on the edge of the village. Its thatch was in poor condition, its door was rickety and its shutters had holes in them, but none of this seemed to worry him.

When Thomas and Caitlin reached the cottage, Emrys was in the garden sitting by a fire. Except when it was raining, this was where they usually found him. Emrys was tall and thin, and the long dark green gown he wore made him look even taller and thinner. His long craggy face, wispy white hair and white beard betrayed his great age. Nobody knew just how old he was, but Thomas and Caitlin's grandmother told them that Emrys had been an old man when her grandfather was a boy. Amazing!

"Hello," said Emrys with a smile, "what brings you here today?"

His voice was thin and hoarse with age.

"We've come to see you; we'd like you to tell us a story," said Caitlin.

Emrys was a kind old man who always had time to tell children stories.

"Which one would you like?"

"One of your stories about King Arthur," replied Thomas.

These stories were Thomas and Caitlin's favourites, and Emrys told them so vividly that you would think he had actually witnessed the events himself. They sat down on a big log close to the fire and Emrys started to tell them a thrilling story about King Arthur and his knights and how, over a hundred years ago, King Arthur had led a huge army out from the great Romano-British fortress of Camulodunum to fight the Saxons. Marching in long columns behind flags depicting a fierce red dragon, Arthur's army had met the Saxon horde and defeated them.

After a while Emrys interrupted the story. "I must visit my neighbour, Old Jonas. He hasn't been well. I won't be long. Wait here. When I come back, I'll finish the story."

They sat and waited. Presently it began to rain, so they went inside the cottage. There was only one room and no upstairs. In that room was Emrys's bed, a table, a bench to sit on, a cooking pot and hung from the rafters that supported the roof, hundreds of bunches of dried herbs of many different kinds. On a shelf attached to the far wall there were several earthenware jars and a few parchment scrolls. They had been in the cottage many times and had often wondered what was in the jars but had never thought to ask.

This time, curiosity got the better of them. Thomas took the lid off one of the jars but recoiled when he saw what was inside.

"Ugh, look at these," he said as he screwed up his face and held his nose.

Caitlin had a quick look. "Yuk, they stink!"

The jar was filled with lots of fishes' shrivelled eyes.

She opened another jar and its contents were almost as bad.

"Ugh, this one's full of frogs' legs."

They opened more jars. Some contained powders or crystals of various colours whilst others contained dried insects, dried worms, bats' wings and other strange items. They were so engrossed looking into the jars they didn't hear the door open. In came Emrys.

"What are you doing?" he snapped.

They were startled and embarrassed at being caught.

"We just wanted to see what was in the jars," murmured Caitlin.

"I hope you haven't eaten anything!"

They were astonished he could think they might actually have eaten such disgusting things.

"Of course not," said Thomas indignantly. "But why do you want these awful things?"

"I use those 'awful things', as you call them, to make medicines. Do you remember the times when you weren't well, and your parents came to me for medicine? Well, each time, I made a mixture of herbs and added one of the powders or other things from the jars. Then I put the mixture into the black pot over the fire, added water and boiled it for a while. When the liquid was cool I gave it you to drink. It might have tasted horrible but it made you feel better, didn't it?"

They were both horrified knowing they had actually drunk something that might have been made from frogs' legs or dried worms and pulled faces.

"How did you learn to make medicines?" queried Caitlin.

"When I was a young man, a famous wizard taught me how to make many of them ... but I have also discovered some myself."

He wanted to change the subject, so he said, "Would you like to see some magic tricks you haven't seen before?"

"Yes!" they chorused.

Emrys was not only a storyteller and a sort of doctor, he was also a magician.

He heated two colourless liquids and mixed them together in a tall narrow vessel made of crystal. At first nothing happened but, very slowly, small yellow flakes formed, dancing and sparkling in the sunlight.

Caitlin gasped in astonishment, "They're beautiful. Are they made of gold?"

Emrys replied mysteriously, "Gold they are, but gold they are not."

Next, he mixed some other colourless liquids in another crystal vessel.

Nothing happened until he waved his hand over the vessel and cast a spell. Saying:

"Water, water, by and by
Show me the colour of the sky."

...followed by some strange words. All at once the liquid turned blue.

As we know, Emrys was good at relating stories. Once he told them a story about a volcano and how, long ago in the land of the Romans, a volcano had buried an entire town with ash.

"Until it erupted," he said, "the people of the town thought the volcano was just an ordinary mountain." This worried Thomas and Caitlin.

Thomas asked, "Do you think one of the mountains surrounding our valley is really a volcano and that one day it will erupt and bury our village in ash?"

Emrys reassured him. "Don't worry, there isn't any danger. There aren't any volcanoes in Britain."

After a pause, he said, "Would you like to see what a volcano is like?"

They didn't like the sound of that.

"No, no. Please don't make a volcano. We don't want to die!" exclaimed Caitlin.

"Oh don't worry, it'll be quite safe. My volcano will be very, very small."

"Are you sure?"

"Very sure. Do you think I want to die?"

They followed him outside, where he heaped up some earth to form a small mound next to the fire. He put some orange powder in a cup and embedded it in the top of the mound. Heating the end of a poker until it was red hot, he plunged it into the powder, chanting:

"Heat and fire
Ash and vapour
Cometh ye forth
By Earth's own labour."

...and again muttered strange words they did not understand.

Red flames and a plume of dark green ash spurted from the centre of the mound. It was very impressive and looked just like the volcano he had described.

"Well, those are all the tricks I have for today," he said. "Now you must go. I have medicines to prepare." He signalled to them to leave.

Chapter 4

The Secret

They left the cottage and went down to the village where some of their friends were playing a game of ball. They enjoyed the game so much that, by the time they set off along the track leading to their cottage, the sun had set and it was rapidly getting dark, too dark to see where they were going. At one point, they strayed from the path and nearly stumbled into a ditch full of water.

Thomas was alarmed. "We've left it too late; it's too dark to get back home. What are we to do?"

Caitlin knew. "We're close to Emrys's cottage. Let's ask if we can stay there until dawn."

They knocked on the door but there was no answer. They knocked again, more loudly. Again there was no answer. Thomas noticed a beam of light streaming through a hole in one of the shutters.

He crept up to it and, putting his eye to the hole, looked through. The inside of the cottage was clearly visible. On the table were two lighted candles, and bent over a long narrow wooden box stood Emrys.

Thomas put his finger to his lips and signalled to Caitlin to come and look. She tip-toed to the window and, finding another hole in the shutter, looked inside. They had often seen the box, which was usually kept locked and standing upright in one corner of the room, but had never seen inside it. Now it was wide open. Emrys reached inside and brought out a long object wrapped in a shiny purple cloak. He placed it on the table very carefully and slowly unwrapped it. They were open-mouthed when they saw what it was; a sword in its scabbard. Not an ordinary sword, like the ones worn by the soldiers at the castle, but a richly decorated one. The hilt and scabbard were decorated with gold and silver and studded with rubies and emeralds.

With a swish of metal against metal, Emrys drew the sword from its scabbard. Its flawless blade glinted in the candlelight. He placed it on the table with its hilt resting on the scabbard and its tip hanging over the edge. Then he laid the purple cloak on the floor, underneath the tip of the sword. Stretching his hands out over the cloak, he muttered strange words. The candles burned more brightly as, very slowly, hundreds of tiny droplets of blood appeared all over the blade. Gathering together they formed larger drops, one of which ran down to the tip and, with a hiss, dripped onto the cloak. More drops followed and, as their number increased, dark shadows started to form and glide around the room. At the same time the sounds of battle could be heard, faint at first but all the time growing louder. The drops continued to fall ... drip ... drip ... drip. More shadows formed and the sounds of battle grew louder. Soon it was a deafening clamour of the shouts and screams of warriors, the neighing of horses and the clash of steel. The shadows took on terrifying shapes and flitted about frantically. The children were petrified but could not take their eyes off the tumultuous scene.

One last large drop of blood gathered on the sword, trickled down the blade and dropped onto the cloak. A cloud of mist rose. Immediately the noise stopped and the candles went out. For a moment, all was dark and silent. Then, with a flash, the candles reignited. In the middle of the room, wearing the purple cloak, now stood a tall bearded knight dressed in chain mail. On the tabard covering his chest was emblazoned a red dragon, and above the dragon, picked out in gold thread, a crown.

Thomas and Caitlin were amazed but also rather frightened and their hearts beat rapidly.

"Where did he come from?" whispered Thomas in a shaky voice.

"I don't know. It must be magic," replied Caitlin.

They continued to watch the knight.

Thomas was becoming ever more curious, "I wonder who he is?"

"I think the crown shows he's a king," replied Caitlin.

Thomas said excitedly, "Perhaps he's King Arthur!"

Emrys bowed to the knight and spoke with him in a strange language. They did not understand the conversation but some of the words seemed to be like the Latin words the priest used in church. As he spoke, Emrys unrolled a parchment and fastened it to the wall opposite the window. Caitlin recognised this parchment because Emrys had once showed it to her and explained that it was a map. On it was drawn their village, the forest, the river and the sea. Emrys and the knight conversed in low voices concerning what was obviously a very serious matter. Every so often they would point to the map and seemed to be particularly interested in an island near the coast.

Eager to see and hear more, Thomas pressed his face against the shutter. To his dismay, it rattled against the window frame. Instantly, Emrys and the knight looked up at the window. Quickly snatching up the sword, Emrys pointed it at the window and shouted a command. A streak of lightning flashed from the sword's point. Thomas and Caitlin, already running away, now found themselves frozen to the spot, quite unable to move. The cottage door opened. Emrys emerged, strode over to them and seized each by an arm. Now their legs began to move again making it possible for him to lead them to the cottage. They expected to see the knight but he had disappeared, leaving the cloak on the floor. However, the beautiful sword and its scabbard were still there.

Emrys was very cross with them for having spied on him.

"Sit on the floor and don't move!" he ordered, a grim look on his face.

They had never seen him so angry and instantly obeyed. Sitting in silence, they wondered what he might do. *'Would he turn them into frogs, or worms or ... perhaps ... murder them!'* They trembled with fright.

While he considered what to do, Emrys sat with his face in his hands and his elbows resting on his knees. After what seemed like an hour, but was actually only a few minutes, he looked up. His face was still grave.

He spoke to them sternly. "You are not to tell anyone what you have seen. It must be kept secret. We will all be in danger if you tell anybody."

"I won't tell, I promise," whispered Caitlin.

"Nor will I," echoed Thomas.

However, Emrys was worried they might be careless and, without thinking, tell someone what they had seen. He had to be sure they would keep it secret. He sat in silence for some minutes staring at them, deep in thought. His stare made them feel uncomfortable.

Then he smiled and said, "I believe you. I know both of you are truthful."

He rose from his chair. "It's late. You must have supper and get some sleep."

He went over to one corner of the room and started to prepare their supper.

While Emrys was doing that, they examined the sword and its scabbard. Close up, it looked even more beautiful and impressive than when seen from a distance. Not only was its hilt jewelled but its blade bore an intricate pattern.

Emrys noticed. "Look but do not touch," he commanded. "It is very sharp."

"Whose sword is it?" asked Caitlin.

"Never you mind," replied Emrys.

"Does it belong to that knight we saw?"

"Oh, you saw the knight, did you?" remarked Emrys gruffly.

"Yes. But where's he gone?"

"Stop asking questions. You shouldn't have been spying on me."

Emrys sounded very annoyed. They sat in silence staring at the floor. Thomas's eyes followed a beetle crawling across the floor. It went under the table and led his gaze to a silver cross.

He nudged Caitlin and whispered, "Look, there's the cross that was pinned on the knight's shoulder. He must have dropped it."

"Quick! Hide it before Emrys notices," she replied. "We can have a good look at it later when he isn't around."

Emrys still had his back to them so Thomas quickly picked it up and put it inside his tunic.

For supper, Emrys gave them each a pear and a cup of water. They wondered where Emrys had got ripe pears from at that time of year but didn't dare ask. The pears were juicy and sweet and they ate them up. During supper, Emrys replaced the sword in its scabbard, wrapped it in the long purple cloak, put it back in the box and locked it. After supper they began to feel very sleepy. Emrys put a big heap of hay on the floor for them to lie on and covered them with a sheepskin blanket.

The crowing of a cock woke them. It was dawn. They opened a shutter and sunlight streamed into the room, together with the odour of fried food. Emrys was already up. He had made a fire outside and was frying eggs.

"Good morning. Did you sleep well?" he enquired.

"Very well," said Thomas.

"Tell me all about last night. I've forgotten why you came to my cottage."

"We went to the village to play with our friends but stayed too late. It was getting dark when we started walking home and we couldn't see where we were going. So, we decided to ask if we could spend the night in your cottage. We knocked on your door and ... and ..."

He paused and screwed up his face. "I can't remember what happened next. I think you gave us supper ... but ... Caitlin, can you remember?"

She frowned. "No ... no ... I ... I can't remember either. I think we just went to bed."

Emrys smiled to himself and didn't ask any more questions. He knew his secret was now completely safe.

Chapter 5

Lost Underground

Thomas and Caitlin thanked Emrys for letting them stay the night and set off home. The path ran along the base of the cliff but above the river, and passed in front of the cave. Although the cave entrance was much taller than a grown man, and wide enough for two people to pass one another, it wasn't readily visible because it was hidden from view by creepers that dangled from the bushes growing on the bank above. Their father and mother had often warned them not to go into the cave because they said it led to a maze of underground passages in which they would soon get lost.

They had also heard stories about monsters that were alleged to live in the forest. Perhaps these monsters also lived in the caves. Every few years, children mysteriously disappeared, never to be seen again. Some people said they had got lost in the underground passages, but others said monsters had eaten them. Thomas and Caitlin didn't know what to believe.

Stopping at the cave's entrance, they peered into the darkness hoping to see something inside, but could not see anything.

Thomas shouted, "Hello!" and, from deep in the earth, there was a faint echo.

The day was hot with no breeze, while the current of air coming from the cave was cool and inviting.

Thomas said, "Let's go just a little way inside. We might find some silver."

But his sister said, "No, we mustn't. Mum and Dad have told us never to go inside because we'll get lost."

"We'll be careful not to get lost," said Thomas.

"No, Thomas. Even if we don't get lost, the monsters will get us."

Thomas was annoyed. "You're always worrying about monsters. They don't exist! Those stories about them aren't true."

Caitlin retorted, "Well, what about the big footprints we saw by the river? What made those?"

"A big bear made them."

He knew the footprints weren't those of a bear but he didn't want to admit it. Caitlin also knew.

She said, "A few years ago Dafydd and Ioan disappeared, and no one knows what happened to them. I think the monsters ate them."

Thomas laughed. "That's rubbish! They probably ran away and got lost, and are now living somewhere else. Anyway, if we only go a little way inside, so we can still see the entrance, we can't possibly get lost."

Caitlin was hot and sweaty, and the coolness of the cave was tempting. She considered Thomas's suggestion and thought it sounded reasonable. '*I wonder what the inside of the cave looks like ... and we might even find some silver ... and the monsters are probably asleep during the day,*' she thought.

Giving in to temptation, she said, "Alright, but we must stop and come back before we lose sight of the entrance."

The dangling creepers brushed their faces as they passed into the cool air of the cave. Immediately, they discovered it was not just a cave but the start of a long dark tunnel. Its sides and roof looked firm and it seemed safe enough so they started walking along it. After about thirty yards, they stopped and looked back. The entrance was clearly visible, and the light from it still lit the way. They continued walking but the further they went the gloomier it became, its walls seeming to close in around them.

To Caitlin it wasn't at all as she had imagined. She began to feel anxious. In the dim light, she imagined hideous faces were staring at her, shapes made by the rough rocks of the tunnel walls. Glancing nervously from wall to wall, she walked on ... but more and more slowly, until finally she came to a halt some way behind Thomas.

"Stop, Thomas, stop!" she shouted.

"Why?"

"Let's go back. There's no silver here," she said in a shaky voice.

Thomas wanted to go on. "Not yet. We've only just started. Don't be scared. Look, you can still see the entrance."

Indeed, it could still be seen, but only as a distant tiny rectangle of light.

An explosion of flapping wings made them jump. Lots of small dark creatures filled the air and flew past their heads. Startled, their hearts skipped a beat before they realised that the creatures were only bats.

The bats made Caitlin even more nervous. "Let's turn back. If we go any further, we won't be able to see the entrance anymore and we'll get lost."

Thomas wasn't listening. He was too interested in the faint greenish glow coming from fungus growing on the walls of the tunnel to take notice of what she was saying.

"Look, this fungus is producing light. It'll be enough for us to see where we are going. Let's go a bit further."

"But you promised not to go too far. You promised to turn back before we lost sight of the entrance."

"You're just scared. You're frightened of your own shadow!" replied Thomas, and he continued walking.

Deeper and deeper into the earth they went, Thomas in front and Caitlin reluctantly following behind, the glow from the fungus providing just enough light for them to see their way. Caitlin continued to plead with Thomas but, after a while, gave up trying to persuade him to turn back. Only the crunch, crunch, crunch of stones beneath their feet broke the silence.

Before long they arrived at a place where the tunnel divided in two. Wondering which way to go, they paused. By now they had rounded a bend and could no longer see the entrance.

"See, Thomas, we don't know which way to go. Let's turn back," said Caitlin.

Thomas ignored her and started walking down the right-hand tunnel. Caitlin followed. However, they soon had to turn back because part of it had collapsed and fallen rocks barred the way ahead. Caitlin was glad. '*Now we'll have to go back,*' she thought. Retracing their steps, they returned to the junction of the two tunnels just as -

Whoosh! ... A sudden gust of wind came up through the left-hand tunnel.

Caitlin thought she heard a faint ghostly voice in the wind saying, *'Danger, danger, go back, go back.'*

"Did you hear that?" she said.

"Hear what?" queried Thomas impatiently.

"I thought I heard a voice telling us to go back."

"I don't believe you; you're making it up."

"No I'm not. Honestly, I heard a voice saying there was danger ahead."

"Well, I heard nothing. I think it was only the sound made by that gust of wind. If you are too scared to come with me, all you need do is go back the way we came."

But Caitlin was becoming more and more certain she really had heard a voice. "It didn't sound like the wind, it sounded like a ghost. Maybe these tunnels are haunted; people say they are. Let's go back!"

Thomas had lost patience with her. He was already walking down the left-hand tunnel. Caitlin hurried after him and soon caught him up.

Many minutes later, they entered a cave about the size of a room in their cottage. In one corner Thomas spotted a small wooden box. He bent down and cautiously opened it. Inside were six candles, a flint, some dried moss and a piece of steel.

"Look what I've found!" he exclaimed. "It's a tinder box. When we want to see better we can use these candles."

He struck the flint against the steel, let the sparks fall on the moss and gently blew until the smouldering moss burst into flames. Caitlin lit a candle. Now they saw what they had not been able to see before ... thousands of tiny sparkling silvery crystals littering the floor.

"Wow," gasped Caitlin, "silver, lots and lots of silver!"

Thomas was doubtful. "I don't think it's silver. It wouldn't have been left here if it was real silver."

"You don't know for sure, Thomas. It might be real silver. I'm going to take some to Emrys. He'll know." She collected a handful of the crystals and put them in the pouch she wore round her waist.

They spied an old ladder fastened to the wall. It went up through a hole in the cave's ceiling into a very dark shaft, dark because its walls had no fungus growing on them. Even the light from a candle could not penetrate the darkness. Looking up, they could not see how tall the ladder was because its top was lost in the darkness.

Thomas grasped the bottom rung. "I wonder where this ladder goes?"

"I don't know or care," said Caitlin sharply. "We've found some silver, so we don't need to go any further. Let's go home."

Thomas ignored her and started climbing the ladder.

Caitlin was alarmed. "Don't go up there. It might be dangerous."

She grabbed his arm but he pulled it away.

Pressing on, and unable to carry a candle, Thomas soon disappeared into total darkness.

"Come back," she shouted in vain. "You don't know what's up there."

Soon, high up, she saw the faint glimmer of a candle flame. He had reached the top. "Come on. It's safe," he shouted.

He didn't tell her that climbing the ladder was difficult and rather dangerous. The ladder had been made for men to climb, and the rungs were too far apart for children.

Caitlin had no option but to follow.

Stepping off the ladder, they found themselves in a long broad gallery illuminated by fungal glow. Out of breath, and with aching arms and legs, they sat on some rocks to rest. For a long time there was complete silence. Then, from deep in the earth, a faint low rumbling noise reached them.

Caitlin jumped up. "What was that?"

Thomas tried to reassure her. "It sounds like falling rocks. I expect rocks fall all the time in these tunnels."

Remembering they had already seen a tunnel where the roof had collapsed, Caitlin was far from reassured. She was shocked by Thomas's calmness.

"Don't say that! If one of the tunnels we've already come through gets blocked, we'll be down here for ever. Nobody will find us and we'll die. Let's go back while we can."

Caitlin's constant requests to turn back now began to have an effect on Thomas, particularly since he too thought they could get trapped.

"Alright, we'll go back. But let's go down this gallery in case there's an easier way to get back down."

"At last!" said Caitlin, feeling relieved. "But no further than the end of the gallery."

They rested a little longer, then walked down the gallery. Soon it crossed a narrow tunnel. At the crossroads they saw dimly a round, white object lying on the ground. Caitlin lit a candle and stooped to examine it. She peered at it, closer ... and closer ... and closer ... but still could not decide what it was. She knocked it with her foot. It rolled over. What a shock! She screamed, dropped the candle and jumped back. Her screams echoed and re-echoed down the gallery. Not thinking where she was going, she ran off down the narrow tunnel.

Thomas ran after her. In their panic they had become careless. Ahead was a hole in the floor of the tunnel.

Bump ... bump ... One after the other, they fell down the hole and into a lower level. Fortunately, something stretched across the hole held them briefly and broke their fall. Whatever it was, it caused them to land gently on the ground below.

Breathlessly, Thomas asked, "Why did you scream and run away? What did you see?"

In a sobbing and trembling voice, Caitlin replied, "It ... it ... it ... was a skull, a little skull ... and it rolled over and grinned at me. It was horrible! Please let's go home. Please, please!"

"Alright, we will," he said.

Then each noticed the other was covered in long pieces of something that looked like thick string. By the light of a candle they examined the 'string' and looked up into the hole.

"What's that?" queried Caitlin in a strangled voice, barely able to speak.

Thomas replied in a trembling, barely-audible voice, "It looks like a spider's web ... but the spider that made it must be huge."

"Spiders have poisonous bites," said Caitlin, almost in tears. "The one that made this web is big enough to kill and eat us."

Anxiously they looked around, fearing the spider might be hiding nearby. Fortunately, it wasn't.

They tried to climb up through the hole. Thomas crouched down and Caitlin sat on his shoulders. When he stood up, Caitlin grabbed the edge of the hole and scrabbled at the rocks with her feet but found them impossible to grip. She dropped down and started to cry.

Between sobs she said, "This is all your fault. You said we wouldn't get lost but now we are lost ... and we might get eaten by a giant spider ... or trapped down here for ever ... or killed by falling rocks." She cried even more.

Thomas put his arm round her shoulders and tried to comfort her, "Come on, let's try to find another way out. I'm sure there must be one."

As he spoke, he saw the pale shape of an animal of some kind far off down the tunnel. It was about the size of a large dog and had probably been attracted by all the noise they had made. *'Was it real or was it a ghost?'* He couldn't tell. Caitlin, who was rubbing her eyes, didn't see it. The animal stood still for a moment, turned its head in their direction and then walked away. Thomas was relieved it had gone and, not wanting to frighten Caitlin even more, he did not tell her about it.

Chapter 6

Almost Drowned

Pocketing some of the 'string', and nervously glancing around in case the spider was hiding nearby, they crept along trying not to make a sound. Up until now, the tunnels had all been tall and dry and had descended quite gradually, but this tunnel was low, round and steep. Its walls were slimy and wet, and a stream of water only a few inches deep flowed along its floor. It was fortunate it was summertime and the weather dry, because in winter, this tunnel was filled with water right up to the roof. The dampness attracted insects and other small creatures. Lots of centipedes and ordinary-sized spiders clung to the walls and hundreds of beetles ran about on the floor.

Splashing through the water, they walked with bent backs. Often they brushed against the sides or the roof. Soon their clothes were covered in slime and squashed insects.

"My back's aching. I'll be glad when we are out of this tunnel," complained Caitlin.

"So will I," added Thomas.

Suddenly Caitlin screamed and shook her hair. "Help! Something's wriggling about in my hair."

She screamed again and beat her tunic with her hands. "Insects! Insects are in my tunic." Again she screamed.

"Oh shut up!" snapped Thomas. He didn't want to hear her complaints because he was having the same trouble.

"I hate this," cried Caitlin.

"So do I," said Thomas, "but there's no other way to go."

The floor of the tunnel was slippery and, several times, they nearly slipped over.

Then Thomas did slip over. Trying to save himself, he caught hold of Caitlin.

"Careful," she shouted, "you'll pull us both down ... aaaagh!"

Splash! Into the slime and water they fell and slid down the tunnel for several yards before coming to a stop against a rock jutting out from its side. For some minutes, they thrashed about in the mire before managing to catch hold of the rock and stagger to their feet.

"Idiot!" said Caitlin crossly. "Look what you've done. Now I'm covered in mud and slime. It's your fault. If you'd listened to me, we wouldn't be here."

"Sorry, I couldn't help slipping over," said Thomas miserably, "... but look, we've almost reached the end of the tunnel."

Caitlin wanted to punish him. "Good ... but thanks to you, I'm all wet and dirty, and my legs are cut and bruised. It's been horrible."

In the silence that followed, the sound of flowing water was heard.

"Listen," said Thomas. "Can you hear that? It sounds like a river."

They walked the last few yards to the end of the tunnel.

"It's a river, an underground river!"

Caitlin was pleased. She knelt down on the bank and dabbled her hand in the rushing water.

"It's freezing," she said.

Shivering from the cold, she took off her tunic, shook out the insects and washed the dirt and slime off herself. Thomas copied.

While washing, Caitlin realised something. "This river must be the Afon Glas. Think how it comes out from under the cliff on the edge of the forest."

Thomas was excited. "If we sail down it, it'll take us home."

"You might be right," said Caitlin, "but how are we to get a boat?"

Thomas's excitement evaporated. They sat on a rock to rest and think.

Now, many times during their journey, they had noticed that some of the tunnel roofs were supported by large thick pieces of wood and that spare pieces often lay scattered around.

After some minutes, Thomas broke the silence. "I know what we can use as a boat. Did you notice pieces of wood lying around in the tunnels? We can use them as floats."

They lit two candles and searched the river bank until they found a timber large enough to carry them both but, try as they might, they did not have enough strength to move it. They searched again and, after further disappointments, found two smaller pieces each big enough to carry one person. Thomas grabbed hold of the end of one of the timbers and tried to drag it to the river. It was very heavy.

"Caitlin, help me!" he shouted.

Using all their strength, they dragged both pieces to the bank of the river and pushed one end of each into the water.

"Lie on it and wrap your arms around it," said Thomas.

"Now push against the bank with your feet."

The timbers partly sank under their weight and only just kept them afloat. Icy cold water soaked into their clothing and lapped against their faces. The cold robbed them of breath and numbed their hands and arms. In less than a minute the river carried them into a low tunnel in which there was only just enough space above the water for their heads and bodies. It was pitch black; they couldn't see anything. They felt afraid and wondered if they had made the right decision ... but there was no way back. The ride was rough, the timbers frequently striking the sides of the tunnel. With each impact they almost lost their grip and often cried out in pain as an arm or a leg got trapped between the timber and the wall.

Hoping she was nearby, and hadn't slipped off her timber, Thomas shouted, "Caitlin, are you alright?"

"Yes, but I can't hold on for much longer."

Thomas was also finding it hard to hold on, and began to fear they would drown before reaching home.

Things were bad and it is difficult to imagine they could be worse, but they became so. The river flowed faster and faster, making their journey rougher and rougher. Waves broke right over their bodies, almost sweeping them off the timbers. They began to hear a deep rumbling sound. At first, it was faint but steadily became louder. With horror, they realised they must be approaching the top of a big waterfall. If they went over it, they would be killed. There was nothing they could do. Nearer and nearer they drifted, going ever faster. The sound of the falling water became a terrible roar. It filled their ears and their minds, making it impossible to think of anything ... except they were going to die!

Near the top of the waterfall the water surged round a large rock situated in the middle of the river. Both timbers struck the rock hard. Whirling round and round under the water, not knowing what was happening, they clung to the timbers for dear life and held their breath. By the time they emerged, they felt their lungs were about to burst. A few minutes longer and they would have drowned.

By good fortune, they had been swept through a completely submerged tunnel into the bottom of a large pool. As each timber rose to the surface it raced across the pool, struck the far bank and wedged itself firmly against it. Half-drowned, they staggered ashore only to collapse from exhaustion.

Wet, cold and bruised they lay on the bank for a long time until, after several hours, Caitlin recovered consciousness. Sitting up, she saw her brother lying motionless on the bank.

She shook him gently. "Thomas, Thomas, are you alright?"

There was no response. Again she shook him, but again there was no response. She felt his face and hands; they were stone cold. She put her ear close to his nose and mouth but could not tell if he was breathing.

Once more she shook him. "Thomas, wake up, please wake up!"

He showed no sign of life. *'Oh no, I think he must be dead,'* she thought. *'Now what am I to do. I'm all alone down here. I'll die, I know I shall.'* She began to cry but, after a while stopped crying and looked at Thomas again. There was no sign of life and he still felt very cold. She had an idea. *'Perhaps he's not dead. If I can make a fire, maybe he'll warm up and be alright.'* She searched among his clothes and found the tinder box. Her heart sank: it was wet but, on opening it slowly and carefully, she was relieved to find it was dry inside.

She dragged Thomas to a large rock and sat him with his back against it. Using splinters of wood, broken off from the timbers lying around, she made a fire. The flames leapt and danced about, lighting up the whole chamber. The sight cheered her. She took off Thomas's tunic and her own clothes and put them over a rock near the fire. While they were drying she warmed her body. After the freezing water of the river, the warmth felt so good.

Only too soon, with no more wood to feed it, the fire began to die down. She placed her hand on Thomas's face and then on his chest. He felt less cold but still showed no sign of life. *'There's no doubt about it, he's dead,'* she thought. In despair, she stood up and walked down the passage towards the deafening sound of the waterfall.

She had almost reached the end of the passage when, mingled with the waterfall's roar, she heard a strange noise. *'What was that? Was it the giant spider?'* She stopped and listened. She heard the noise again, from somewhere behind her. *'Perhaps the spider has come to eat Thomas,'* she thought. She froze. Shaking with fear, her heart thundering, she slowly turned and looked back. No spider was in sight, only Thomas's body ... just visible in the faint light of the dying fire. *'Perhaps it's hiding,'* she thought. She stooped down and watched. Minutes passed but nothing happened. She decided to take a chance and hide his body under some stones. Looking around, she cautiously approached the body. There was still no sign of the spider.

When she had almost reached Thomas, the noise came again. Her heart leapt, not with fear but with delight. It was Thomas who was making the noise; he was groaning. She knelt down beside him and placed a hand on his brow. It was warm. He stirred and opened his eyes. Caitlin was overjoyed. Tears of happiness rolled down her cheeks as she hugged and hugged him.

"Oh, Thomas you're alive, you're alive. I thought you were dead."

"Of course I'm alive," said Thomas weakly. "Help me sit up."

They sat clinging to one another for a long time before they spoke.

"Thomas, we can't go on that river again, even if it is the Afon Glas. We were lucky not to drown. We'll have to find another way out of here. If we don't, we'll die." She began to cry again.

Thomas took her hands in his and said, "Don't worry, there must be another way out and I'm sure we'll find it."

Caitlin sighed. "You said that before, just after we fell through the spider's web, but look what's happened to us now."

Thomas was also worried. He was beginning to think they might never escape from the tunnels, but he was determined not to let his sister know of his doubts.

Chapter 7

The Monster and the Spider

They hurried down the tunnel leading from the pool to the waterfall. Thomas moved too quickly and nearly went over the edge of a high cliff.

"Whoa!" he said as he swayed backwards and forwards on its edge. Quickly he stepped back into the passage.

Caitlin craned her neck to look. The view made her dizzy.

They were halfway up the side of an enormous cavern, so big a church and its steeple could easily have fitted inside it. It was gloomy but not completely dark because, through a small opening in its roof, some daylight streamed. They looked up at the opening and were dismayed to see silk-wrapped bodies of small birds hanging in giant cobwebs. Neither said anything; they dared not think about the spider or where it might be hiding.

The waterfall that had almost claimed their lives was immense. A broad torrent of glistening water emerged from the end of a broad tunnel close to the cavern's roof and fell into the black depths below with a noise like thunder. Clouds of spray filled the air, the cold droplets showering their faces. They stared at the waterfall, overwhelmed by its size. How lucky they were not to have been swept over its lip!

From where they stood, a narrow ledge, cut into the rock, went along the wall of the cavern and behind the waterfall. Caitlin glanced right and left.

The prospect worried her. "I don't fancy going along that ledge, it's so narrow."

"There's no other way," said Thomas. "We'll have to go along it. Follow me ... but don't look down."

The ledge was wet and slippery. With their backs pressed against the rock face, they moved sideways along it, one step at a time, slowly making their way towards the waterfall. The further they went the more frightened they became, fearing that at any moment they might slip and fall to their deaths in the black void below. After a few yards, they encountered a part of the ledge that sloped towards the big drop. With each step, their feet slid forwards.

"I can't go on," whimpered Caitlin, eyes closed, hands pressed against the rock.

Thomas took her hand. "Hold tight and keep going."

Soon, drenched with water, they were very close to the waterfall. Suddenly, Thomas's feet slid from under him. He let go of Caitlin's hand, landed on the ledge on his bottom and started to slide forwards. At that exact moment, something like a long whip whistled through the air, wrapped itself around his waist and dragged him behind the falling water. Caitlin was panic-stricken. She screamed but, in a matter of seconds, was also seized.

The 'whip' belonged to a monster who lived in a cave behind the waterfall. As each was drawn into the cave, the monster deposited them on a large mound of hay situated in one corner. Next to this mound was an empty wooden cage, very like one that had been stolen from their farm one night. The monster used this cage to imprison animals it had caught ... until it was ready to eat them!

Recovering from their fright, they saw their captor; a large slim dark-green lizard. It had a black horn on its head, rather like that of a rhinoceros only longer, and four legs of almost equal size. Its black tail was very long and thin and this is what it had used to seize them.

66

With its yellow slit eyes, the monster looked closely at Thomas and then at Caitlin, its long red forked tongue constantly darting in and out of its yellow-green slime-dripping mouth. The overpowering stench of its breath made them feel sick; it smelt worse than the pig manure in their farmyard. Now and then it growled, raising its lips to expose a set of long sharp curved teeth. Feeling its rough cold wet tongue lick their faces, they whimpered with fear thinking they were about to be eaten. Fortunately, the monster had recently eaten a lamb and wasn't hungry. It decided to eat them some other day, when it was unable to catch anything in the world above. Thrusting them into the cage, it secured the door by pushing a large rock against it. Then it lay down on the hay and went to sleep.

Hundreds of bones lay scattered across the cave floor and more were heaped up next to the hay. Caitlin stared at the heap and spotted a couple of small skulls.

In a small fearful voice she said, "Thomas, see those skulls? They're not children's skulls, are they?"

Horrified, Thomas swallowed hard before he replied. "No ... I don't think so," he lied. "I think they're ... erm ... badgers' skulls." He didn't sound convincing.

"I hope you're right," she said. "If you're wrong, it won't be long before our skulls join them."

Thomas knew they were children's skulls ... *'they might even be those of Dafydd and Ioan,'* he thought ... but he didn't want to admit it, despite noticing the torn remains of some small clothes mixed with the hay.

Soaking wet, they huddled together on some hay in one corner of the cage, shivering partly from feeling cold but more from fear. They were very tired. Eventually, out of sheer exhaustion, they must have fallen asleep, because the next thing they knew was being woken by the monster pushing apples and a bowl of water through the bars of their cage. Not having eaten for over a day, they were very hungry and thirsty, and quickly ate the apples and drank the water.

The monster spent most of its time away from the cave searching for food. When it was absent they made efforts to escape. They tried to squeeze through the bars but they were too close together. They tried to loosen the bars, but did not succeed. They tried to push open the door but it was too firmly secured. They hammered on the roof with their fists, but it was very strong. They even thought of digging a tunnel with their bare hands but, when they examined the floor of the cage, they found it was placed on solid rock.

Whenever the monster returned, it brought food for itself and some for them. Its own meals consisted almost entirely of raw meat but it never gave them any. They were glad about that, but got bored eating only carrots, raw cabbage and apples. Apart from providing them with food, the monster ignored them and spent its time in the cave either eating or sleeping.

On one occasion it returned from an expedition looking rather battered, having acquired a large wound on its front right leg. Obviously it had fought some other large creature. After some time, probably a few days, Thomas noticed the wound was becoming painful because the monster groaned and licked it repeatedly. It appeared to be infected and looked as though it was filled with pus. Soon the monster stopped leaving the cave, lay on the hay and hardly moved. It was sick. Day after day, they watched it becoming weaker and weaker.

Thomas said gleefully, "I think it's going to die ... and a good thing too!"

Caitlin was more thoughtful. Looking serious, she said, "I hope it doesn't die."

Thomas was astonished. "Why? If it dies then it can't eat us."

"Well, if it dies, we'll die too ... because we'll never be able to escape from this cage. We've got to think how we can keep it alive."

Thomas was shocked ... he hadn't thought of that.

Caitlin continued, "If we can think of a way to heal its wound, the monster will live. It might even be grateful and let us go." They sat and thought how they might do this.

Shortly, Caitlin reminded Thomas of something that once happened to her.

"Do you remember the time we were playing in the river when I fell and grazed my leg on a sharp rock?"

"Ye... es."

"Well the wound didn't heal. It became inflamed making me felt unwell. Dad took me on the donkey to see Emrys who put some dried fungus on the wound and tied a bandage round it. After a few days I felt better. Soon afterwards, the wound healed up."

"But we haven't got any of Emrys's medicines here," objected Thomas.

"That's true. But lots of fungus is growing on the walls of this cave. Perhaps it's the same fungus Emrys used. If we can get the monster to understand us, we can try treating its wound the same way."

Thomas stood up, held onto the bars and shouted loudly, "If we make your wound better will you let us go?"

The monster was startled, looked up quickly and stared at him. Unable to speak, it could not reply. To try to show it what he meant, Thomas held up his right arm, made a moaning noise and licked it. The monster's curiosity was aroused. It limped over to the cage, held up the leg with the wound and flicked its tongue at him. Thomas nodded, stroked his right arm with his left hand, wrapped some hay around it and smiled. Puzzled, the monster opened the cage door and let them out but, to make sure they didn't escape, it stood blocking the cave's entrance. As they went round the cave scraping handfuls of fungus off the walls, the monster eyed them suspiciously. Having applied fungus to the wound, they covered it with plenty of hay and tied a piece of the spider's silk round it. The monster looked at what they had done and roared. Growling and lashing its tail about, it advanced and drove them back into the cage, pushed the stone against the door, and lay down on the hay.

Time passed. They had now lost all track of the days and did not know how long they'd been underground. After what they thought was a few days, the monster began to feel better and let them out of the cage again so they could put fresh fungus on the wound.

One morning they awoke to find the monster missing. Later it returned carrying a dead deer. It had started hunting again. The wound must have healed. However, the monster kept the wound covered and would not allow them to see it. Then it made a mistake ... when it thought they were asleep, it uncovered the wound. Unfortunately for the monster, Caitlin was not asleep.

She woke her brother. "Thomas, I've just seen the monster's leg. The wound has healed. Now it should let us go."

Thomas stood up, smacked his right arm and shouted loudly, "Your wound has healed. Let us go!" The monster seemed to understand because it lowered its head, growled and turned its back on him.

More time passed and they continued to press the monster to set them free but, each time, it just ignored them. They began to despair.

Caitlin said, "I don't think the monster will ever let us go. I think it's keeping us for when it can't find any food."

Thomas agreed. "I think you're right," he said gloomily.

However, help was to arrive in an unexpected form.

Sometime later, the monster was absent for longer than usual.

Caitlin remarked, "I hope the monster comes back soon. We've only got two apples and a little water left."

Thomas was just as worried. "If it's dead, we'll soon die too."

At long last they heard a soft pattering sound near the cave's entrance.

"It's coming back!" exclaimed Thomas.

But they both stared open-mouthed when they saw what was entering the cave from above the entrance. It was a giant white spider! It must have known the monster wasn't present and sensed that live food (in the form of Thomas and Caitlin) was to be found in the cave. They were petrified because they knew they would make it an excellent meal.

The spider raised its striped black and white front legs and looked around with its two large shining red eyes and its many smaller black ones. Slowly it came towards the cage.

Caitlin whispered, "Keep perfectly still. It mightn't see us."

They kept still and held their breath ... but it made no difference. The spider came right up to the cage. Snapping its sharp shiny black fangs, it walked round the cage looking for a way in. Every now and then, in the hope of catching one of them, it thrust a leg through the bars but always failed because they quickly darted out of the way. Having walked all round the cage and discovered that there was no way in, it started to chew through one of the bars.

Caitlin recognised an opportunity and, in a tremulous voice, said, "This might be the only chance we'll ever get to escape. Wait until it has chewed right through the bar, then run like mad through the gap."

With rapidly beating hearts they waited. As soon as the bar was severed, they rushed through the gap and raced for the cave entrance. Now, as you know, spiders can run very quickly and this one was soon catching them up. They tried to run faster but, because they were frightened, their legs felt like lead and wouldn't move fast enough. Closer and closer it came. Thomas felt one of its claws touch his back. What was he to do?

Nearby was a jumbled heap of huge slabs of stone. Long ago, these had fallen from the cave's roof. Thomas came to a sudden halt near the stones and turned round. The spider was almost on him. He ran back underneath it. This surprised the spider. It too turned but was not quick enough to prevent him slipping into one of the spaces between the slabs. Thomas's trick gave Caitlin time to hide.

The spider wasn't going to give up. Positioning itself over the heap, it tried to capture him by pushing one of its front legs into the space where he was hiding. Thomas picked up a large stone and struck the spider's leg. The spider emitted a shrill scream, withdrew its leg but stayed put. Now they were stuck. They became hungrier and thirstier by the hour but the spider showed no sign of moving. They were worried because they had often seen normal-sized spiders sitting in the middle of their webs for days without moving. The possible return of the monster was their only hope and they prayed for it to come back.

Just when they had almost given up hope, and were weak from lack of food and water, the spider suddenly moved away. Cautiously, they poked their heads out and immediately saw the reason. Standing in the entrance was the monster, holding a dead pig in its jaws. The moment it saw its old enemy, it dropped the pig and roared loudly. Rushing at the spider, it dug its horn into the spider's side and wrapped its tail around the spider's body. The spider uttered a horrible scream, clamped its fangs round the monster's neck and started to wrap the monster in thick silken threads. The two were locked together. Making terrible screeching noises, over and over they rolled, biting and clawing, legs and tail flailing. Thomas and Caitlin didn't stop to watch but made good their escape.

Chapter 8

Blue Fish

With trepidation, they realised that once more they would have to go along the narrow ledge. However, this part of the ledge was a bit wider than the section along which they had come.

"Crawl... it'll be safer," said Thomas.

He got down on his hands and knees and Caitlin copied. Trembling and sweating with fear, they crawled along as quickly as they dared until they reached the entrance to another tunnel. They did not know where this tunnel might take them and they did not care. Their only thought was to get as far away as possible from the monster and the spider. *'Were they still fighting one another?'* They did not know because the noise of the waterfall had long blocked out the sounds of the struggle.

Occasionally stumbling and falling over, they raced along the tunnel until their legs ached and they were quite out of breath.

"I'm tired out, I can't go any further," panted Caitlin. "Let's stop and rest."

They sat down on some rocks and listened for sounds that would warn them of the approach of the monster or the spider. All was quiet save for the sound of water dripping into a pool somewhere ahead of them: plop ... plop ... plop ... plop... The sound was restful and they began to forget they might still be in danger until Thomas abruptly jumped up.

"Come on, let's go! Whoever has won the fight might be after us," he shouted.

Hurrying along the passageway and rounding a bend, they entered a vast cavern, unlike any they had come across before. In the floor of the cavern was a lake whose water radiated a faint blue light. Hundreds of long thin white stalactites hung from the roof and the overhanging rocks, while similar stalagmites reached up from the floor. Some of the stalactites and stalagmites had joined together and formed beautiful ribbed columns, scores of which lined the cavern's walls. All glowed dimly with the pale green light of the fungus but also sparkled with thousands of tiny twinkling lights. Their eyes followed the columns up to a ceiling that looked like the star-filled sky of a dark winter's night. It was a magical scene. The sight took their breath away, a sight enhanced by its reflection in the mirror-like surface of the lake. Entranced by the beauty of the scene they stood staring at it for several minutes, motionless and in silence.

Suddenly, fluorescent green ripples spread across the water and a large silvery-blue fish, with silver fins and a pale blue tail, leapt repeatedly in and out of the water as it rapidly made its way towards them. Fearing the fish might be just as dangerous as the green monster or the spider, Thomas and Caitlin backed away. The fish swam the last few yards to where they were standing, pushed its head out of the water and stared at them. At that moment, Caitlin felt a tingling inside her head. She put her hands up to her head and then noticed Thomas was doing the same.

To their amazement, they both heard the fish say, "Don't be afraid. I won't hurt you." They were astonished that a fish could speak, particularly since it didn't seem to be moving its mouth. It didn't look fierce so they relaxed a little, but still didn't trust it.

"Are you speaking to us, fish?" asked Caitlin, scarcely able to believe it.

"Yes. I can see from the way you are holding your heads that you are hearing me."

"But you are speaking without moving your mouth," said Thomas.

"I cannot speak like you do, my mouth is the wrong shape. You think you hear me speak, but it's not with your ears that you hear me. Instead, I send my thoughts straight to your minds. It's a gift given to me long ago by a magician to enable me to speak to him. Now tell me who you are and how you got here. Nobody from outside, except the magician, has ever visited this lake."

They took it in turns to tell the fish the whole story.

"You were unlucky to have met Voran," said the fish. "Most of the creatures who live in these tunnels are harmless. Only Voran and Spider and their relatives will harm you."

Caitlin said, "We don't want to be down here. We want to go home but we don't know how to escape. Please help us."

"There are only three ways to reach this lake," replied the fish, "and those are the same ways to escape from it. Each is well-defended; the first by the waterfall, the second by the two-headed snake and the third by the lava chamber. You are the only people to have got past the waterfall and are extremely lucky to have survived."

She paused, stared at them as if unable to believe they were really there, then continued, "You mentioned coming down a round tunnel coated in slime. That must have been one of the burrows made by the Worm. The large tunnels are workings from the old Roman silver mines but the narrow round burrows are made by the Worm."

"The Worm must be very big to make such burrows," said Caitlin.

"Certainly... but most creatures down here are enormous."

"Is the Worm dangerous? Will it harm us?" asked Thomas.

"The Worm is quite harmless but its burrowing does make a terrible mess and its burrows can sometimes be a nuisance. However, the Worm is also useful because, when it wants to have a sleep, it makes a cave in the side of its burrow big enough for it to curl up in. Many who live down here use these caves as homes, particularly the dragons."

"Dragons!" exclaimed Caitlin in alarm.

"Oh yes. There are dragons down here too, but they are my friends. They won't harm you. If you meet them, just say Blue Fish is your friend."

"Will they understand?"

"Yes ... in the same way I understand you."

Despite her friendliness, Blue Fish was suspicious. *How have they managed to survive the waterfall? In hundreds of years nobody else has survived it. Perhaps they are spies sent by my enemies ... even by the witch. I shall have them tested.*

She gave them directions on how to escape from the tunnels, but warned they would have to pass the two-headed snake.

"One head senses the good in a person and the other senses the evil. If a person intends no harm the snake lets them pass, but if they have wicked deeds in mind the snake wraps itself around them, squeezes the life out of them and swallows them."

She studied their faces, searching for a reaction that might betray them, but saw nothing suspicious.

Thomas whispered to Caitlin, "I'm not planning to do anything wicked, are you?"

"Of course not!"

"Well, we've nothing to fear.'

"Maybe, but I don't like the thought of meeting a giant snake."

"Nor me ... but that's the way we've got to go."

Just as they were about to leave, Caitlin, curious as ever, looked closely at one of the twinkling lights and discovered that it belonged to a glow worm. This gave her an idea. In her pouch she had an old glass bottle which she had found when they first entered the cave. She collected several glow-worms and put them in the bottle. The bottle was now a lamp whose light would help them find their way in the gloom. It would take the place of the candles, which had all been used up.

As they waved goodbye, Blue Fish said, "Remember, stick to the old mine workings and always try to walk uphill."

Taking a broad tunnel on the far side of the lake, they started their journey to the surface. For the first time since they entered the caves they felt cheerful. Walking along, they chatted about Blue Fish.

"I wonder how Blue Fish came to live underground," mused Caitlin. "It's a strange place for a fish to live ... and how does she know her way through the tunnels?"

"Perhaps the magician told her," said Thomas.

"I wonder who he is? Do you think he's Emrys?"

After they had walked for about a mile, they saw two glowing red spots moving about in the darkness ahead.

Caitlin was alarmed. "What are those? They look like eyes."

Thomas started to pant with fear. "They're the Devil's eyes; he's waiting for us!"

He turned to run away but Caitlin grabbed his arm. "Calm down. It's not the Devil, it's the two-headed snake."

In great dread, they walked slowly towards the red spots. They knew they had to pass the snake. Coming closer, they saw its mottled brown body, as thick as a tree trunk, coiled up in the passageway with its heads poised above the coils. One head was looking their way and the other in the opposite direction. At their approach the snake turned both heads towards them and hissed loudly. They paused, absolutely terrified, wanting to run away, but were so frightened they were unable to move. The coils of the snake's body slowly slid past one another as it wrapped itself round Thomas's legs and then round his body. Gripping him tightly, it scanned his face with its luminous red eyes while its forked tongues darted in and out of its mouths as it flicked them over his forehead and tasted his thoughts. Thomas was frightened ... and worried ... because, a few days before they entered the tunnels, he had quarrelled with Caitlin and spitefully buried her doll in the manure heap. *'The snake would find out. Perhaps it would eat him!'* His heart pounded in his chest as he shivered with fright.

However, the snake must not have thought it a serious offence because it soon let him go. Caitlin was relieved to see her brother released but her relief was brief because she too was immediately seized. She screamed but the snake took no notice and examined her in the same way it had examined Thomas. Satisfied that neither had any evil intentions it drew back, rested its heads on its coils and let them pass.

They hurried away and had not gone very far when Caitlin said, "I had no idea what happened to my doll, but now I know." She glared at Thomas who hung his head in shame.

"I'm sorry," he said. "It was a nasty thing to do. When we get out of here I'll make you a new doll."

After a while, they came to a place where the tunnel started to ascend quite steeply. Thomas remembered what Blue Fish had said about always following tunnels that went uphill.

He was excited. "Look Caitlin, the tunnel's going up."

"So it is. It must be heading for the surface. We'll soon be out of here. Hurray!"

They were elated. Very soon they would be out in the fresh air ... but it was not to be. Without warning, the earth around them shook violently and started to break up.

"It's an earthquake!" shouted Thomas. "We'll be crushed to death."

They crouched down and covered their heads with their hands. Some way ahead, lots of rocks tumbled into the tunnel and a great cloud of dust surged towards them. Hardly able to breathe, they coughed and coughed. As suddenly as it had begun, it stopped. When enough dust had settled for them to see what had happened, they ran to the fallen rocks and held up their lamp. To their dismay, they saw the tunnel they were following was now blocked.

Through a gap in the fallen rocks, Thomas glimpsed something pink and fleshy.

"It's the Worm Blue Fish told us about. It's huge, even bigger than I imagined."

"Let's see," said Caitlin. She too was astonished by its size.

"So it wasn't an earthquake. It was the Worm making a burrow. But how are we to get past it? It's blocking the way."

"Perhaps it'll soon move on. Let's wait and see," said Thomas.

Soon a ripple spread along the worm's body as it moved forward, but the distance it moved was very small indeed, only one or two inches.

"Did you see that?" said Thomas. "It moved, but hardly at all. We're going to have to wait a long, long time."

"Well, we've no alternative," observed Caitlin.

They sat on the rubble and resigned themselves to a long wait. Well, it was a long wait. It must have been several hours before the end of the Worm's tail finally slid past the gap. They looked across the width of the Worm's burrow, hoping to see their tunnel continuing on the other side but were disappointed; it was completely blocked by fallen rocks. To catch sight of the Worm was exciting but, as Blue Fish had warned, its burrowing could be a nuisance. In fact, it was more than a nuisance because it was now impossible for them to continue their journey.

"What are we to do? The Worm has filled our tunnel with rubble. We can't go on," said Caitlin."

The new burrow the Worm had made was about a yard in diameter, its sides covered in fresh worm slime. Thomas climbed through the gap and into the burrow. He looked along it in the direction of the Worm and held up the glow worm lamp. The Worm's tail looked pink and moist, just like that of an ordinary earthworm only very much bigger. For a while he watched the Worm, but then he noticed that the burrow's walls were not made of solid rock but of clay mixed with stones.

"Caitlin, come and see what I've discovered." She quickly scrambled into the burrow.

"Look!" he cried, pulling handfuls of clay from the burrow's walls.

"Of course." said Caitlin. "A worm wouldn't be able to burrow through solid rock ... and you often get clay near the surface. If we follow the Worm it'll eventually go up to the surface."

"Why d'you think that?"

"Well, every so often, worms have to go up to the surface to get rid of the earth they've eaten. Do you remember the big mounds of earth and clay in the forest? I think they're giant worm casts."

"But there's a problem," continued Caitlin. "The Worm moves so slowly we might starve to death before it next goes to the surface."

Their excitement evaporated. They stood in silence, wondering what to do.

Thomas said, "I know. Let's follow the burrow the way the Worm has already come. Perhaps it has recently been to the surface."

With bent backs, they walked along the burrow but found it heavy going because the worm slime was like glue and stuck to their feet. This slime lifted clay and stones from the floor of the burrow forming an enormous ball of earth on each foot. It felt as though they were wearing big boots made of lead. Each step was a great effort. Occasionally they rested, but not for long because they were determined to press on. Soon their hopes were dashed because, after a few hundred yards, the burrow started to descend.

"It's hopeless," said Thomas. "We might follow this burrow for miles and still not reach the surface. We'd better go back to where Blue Fish lives."

Feeling depressed, they struggled through the slime back to the opening in the side of the burrow. After freeing their feet from the balls of earth, they wearily tramped along the tunnel in the direction of Blue Fish's lake. Once more they would have to pass the two-headed snake and did not relish the idea of being examined yet again. At their approach, the snake raised its heads, hissed and tasted the air but, because it had already met them, it settled down immediately and let them pass by.

Chapter 9

Unanswered Questions

They had almost reached the lake when Caitlin heard something.

"Stop. I think I can hear voices."

The sound seemed to be coming from a narrow cleft in the wall of the tunnel.

They stood in silence and listened.

Thomas nodded. "You're right. They're coming from that cleft in the rock."

They had passed this way before but, because they were then facing in the opposite direction, the cleft had been hidden from their view.

Curious, they squeezed through the cleft and came out near the top of a high circular grotto partly filled with thousands of large pointed glass-like crystals. A huge chandelier bearing hundreds of candles hung from the centre of the ceiling. Its light,

89

reflected back and forth between the crystals, made the whole grotto blaze with light. Near the top of the walls, a number of poles stuck out. Hung from these were large banners, each depicting a fierce-looking red dragon on a green background. Each dragon held a shield, and each shield bore a different coat of arms. The banners were stained and tattered, as if they had been carried in battle.

From where they were standing, a long steep flight of steps wound its way among the crystals down to the floor below, where a number of dark figures sat in a circle. The dazzling light made it hard to see what they looked like. It seemed they were arguing about something, because the sound of their low gruff voices kept rising and falling.

"What are they saying?" whispered Thomas.

"I don't know. Let's try to get closer," replied Caitlin.

With Caitlin leading the way, they tiptoed very quietly down the steps.

A short way down, Caitlin stopped and whispered, "If we get any closer they'll see us. We'd better hide".

They crouched down behind an extra-large mass of crystals, and watched and listened. Now they could see the men more clearly. All were wearing chain mail and most were bearded.

The arguing continued for some time and seemed to be concerned with something shown on a map spread out on the table. Eventually, they seemed to reach agreement because their voices died down. Their leader stood and rolled up the map.

All rose from their seats, bowed and followed him, chanting over and over again, "Arturus, Arturus, Britannia omnia rex ... Arturus, Arturus, Britannia omnia rex ..." The whole chamber echoed and re-echoed with the chanting.

Thomas and Caitlin watched them walk off into the shadows. Then they were gone and all was silent. The chamber seemed completely empty.

"D'you think they've gone?" asked Thomas.

"I think so ... but we should wait before we move just in case they come back."

When they were sure the men were not going to reappear, Thomas said, "Let's go down to the bottom and see if we can find where they went."

Cautiously they descended the steps, stopping every now and then to make sure they were not being watched. At the bottom was a large round table made of polished black granite surrounded by curved benches made of the same stone. The top of the table bore a large elaborately-carved letter A. Below the letter was inscribed a crossed sword and scabbard and above it a crowned dragon, all inlaid with gold.

Taking the same path the men had taken, they came to a stout wooden door hidden in the shadows. It was firmly secured by two large bolts the size of a man's forearm, each locked with an enormous iron lock.

"They must have gone through here," said Thomas.

Caitlin was more observant. "They can't have done. The door's locked on this side. If they'd gone through it, it would have been locked on the other side. Anyway, everything's very rusty. This door hasn't been opened for years." It was puzzling.

"Well, wherever they've gone, we'd better not stay long in case they come back and aren't friendly," remarked Thomas.

Caitlin agreed. Hurrying up the steps, they slipped through the cleft and back into the tunnel.

Tired, thirsty and hungry they continued on their way and, at long last, arrived at the lake. Blue Fish was having a meal of shrimps and insect larvae and didn't seem at all surprised to see them.

"Hello," she said. "Are you hungry?"

They wondered why she didn't ask about their return but they told her about the Worm and how it had blocked the exit tunnel. She did not comment.

They also told her about their discovery of the crystal grotto and of the men they had seen.

"Do you know who those men are?" asked Caitlin.

"Would you like something to eat?" said Blue Fish.

Caitlin repeated her question.

"Do have some shrimps," said Blue Fish.

"Thank you," they said and ate the shrimps, even though they hadn't been cooked.

"Why won't you answer our questions?" demanded Thomas.

"Try some insect larvae. They're delicious," said Blue Fish

"No thank you!" they snapped, cross because she wouldn't answer their questions.

It was obvious Blue Fish was hiding something. This aroused their curiosity even more, but they were too exhausted to try to question her further, and soon fell asleep on a large flat rock by the side of the lake.

Many hours later they awoke, feeling stiff but refreshed. Looking across the lake, they saw something they hadn't noticed before. On the far side was a door set in an archway made of properly cut and shaped stones. It was almost identical to the door they had seen in the grotto, except it bore a large Celtic cross made of silver. Three broad stone steps led from the door down to the water's edge. Clearly, the door could only be reached by boat. They asked Blue Fish what was on the other side of the door, but she ignored their question and swam to the far side of the lake.

When she returned she said, "I think both of you are trustworthy young humans. If you weren't, the two-headed snake wouldn't have let you pass. So, I have decided to entrust you with an important mission. During your journey back home, the purpose of the mission will be revealed ... but only when you know the answer to this riddle."

She chanted the riddle and made them repeat it.

"When three times three
Are like the leaves of a tree
Then a favour granted
Must be repaid."

Satisfied they had memorised it, she said, "Now the Worm has blocked the snake's tunnel, there's only one other way out. This other route is longer and more dangerous, because it takes you through a lava chamber. To cross it safely, you must follow my instructions." They listened intently.

Finally she said, "Before you go I have something to give you."

She dived to the bottom of the pool and came up bearing a pearl the size of a cherry which she gave to Caitlin.

"Do not lose this pearl. If anyone challenges you, show it them. It will keep you safe."

She paused and then added, "If I have misjudged you and you prove unworthy of the task I have set, you will not understand the riddle and my pearl will turn to dust."

They looked carefully at the pearl. Like her, it was a beautiful silvery blue but, when turned in the light, it shimmered with all the colours of the rainbow. Caitlin put it in the bottom of her pouch and fastened the button on the flap. They thanked Blue Fish, said goodbye and once more set off.

Chapter 10

The Red Dragon

After a seemingly endless tramp, they felt hot air streaming down the tunnel, and knew they must be approaching the lava chamber. The final few yards of the tunnel descended steeply before arriving at the bottom of a low broad chamber filled with hot choking fumes. Light from a pool of red-hot lava set in its middle illuminated the whole chamber. Up until now, the walls of the caves they had passed through had all been roughly-hewn, but the walls of this chamber were smooth, made so by the constant swirl of red-hot lava. It was difficult to breathe and so hot they felt their clothes might catch fire and their faces burn. However, they knew that if they were ever to get back home, they must cross this chamber.

As they watched, the pool slowly grew in size as more and more lava, seething and bubbling with the hot suffocating gases escaping from it, welled up from deep in the earth. Blue Fish had told them that every few hours lava filled the whole chamber ... right up to the ceiling. She had also warned them not to try to cross it until an eruption had completely finished, the lava drained away and the floor had cooled down. Heeding the fish's advice, they waited. The lava rose and rose. The heat became unbearable causing them to retreat back along the tunnel. Hours passed while the eruption took place but eventually they noticed a change; the air did not seem quite so hot.

"Let's see if the eruption's finished," suggested Caitlin, fed up with the long wait.

It had finished and almost all the lava had drained away. Only a small pool was left. The floor was red hot; too hot even to watch. They went away and came back later. The floor no longer glowed and they wondered if it was safe to cross.

"Caitlin, do you think it's cool enough?"

"We need to be sure," she replied. "We don't want to get burned ... but I know how to find out." Plucking a few threads from a tear in her tunic, she threw them onto the floor. Immediately they burst into flames.

They waited and waited for it to cool further until Thomas said impatiently, "We can't wait for ever. Test it again." This time, the threads turned black but did not burn.

"It's still very hot," said Caitlin, "but we'll have to cross. If we wait any longer, the next eruption will begin."

Gasping and coughing from breathing in the fumes hanging in the air, they ran quickly across the floor to the other side. The smell of charred wood mingled with the fumes. The wooden soles of their shoes had been singed, but they had managed to cross safely.

Loud chattering laughter suddenly filled the chamber, and died away just as quickly as it had started. They were startled.

"Where did that laughter come from?" asked Caitlin rather nervously.

They looked around but there was nobody in sight.

"I don't know, but I don't like it," said Thomas. They hurried on.

All was now silent, save for the sound of their own footsteps and the increasingly distant gurgling of the lava. After a while, they heard a sort of deep growling noise.

Caitlin whispered, "What's that?"

"I hope it's not Voran," said Thomas. "Perhaps we should turn back."

Caitlin clutched the pearl. "No! Blue Fish told us this was the way to go and she gave me the pearl to keep us safe."

They crept along while the growling noise became louder and louder.

The noise was coming from a small cave in the side of the tunnel. It was loud and frightening but didn't sound like Voran. With his back against the tunnel wall, Thomas edged along to the cave entrance. Peering round the side, he was surprised to see a very large red dragon, fast asleep and snoring loudly. It's long, scaly tail was wrapped round its body, its leathery wings folded over its back and its head was resting on its front feet.

They started to creep across the cave entrance, hoping not to wake the dragon ... but failed. With a mighty roar, it rose to its feet and shot a huge jet of flame at them. Narrowly missing them, it singed their hair. They screamed and quickly retreated.

The dragon advanced and shouted, "Try to attack me while I was sleeping, would you. I'll teach you a lesson, you wretched midgets. I'm going to set you both on fire, and send your blackened bones to your master!" He breathed more fire but they jumped back out of the way.

In a trembling voice, Thomas whimpered, "Please don't burn us. We mean no harm. We are lost. We weren't trying to attack you. How could we harm someone as big as you?"

The dragon lowered his head and looked at them intently. *'They are very small. They've no weapons and don't look harmful,'* he thought.

"Are you sure Voran didn't send you?" asked the dragon suspiciously.

"No!" replied Caitlin. "Voran is our enemy too. He caught us, kept us in a cage and was planning to eat us ... but we escaped."

The dragon snorted, making the little flames that played around his nostrils burn a bit brighter. *'Her story sounds convincing; it's just the sort of thing Voran would do,'* he thought.

Gradually he calmed down and stopped breathing fire.

"Who are you and how did you get here?" he asked.

They told him the whole story. Caitlin then thought to show him the pearl that Blue Fish had given her.

At the sight of the pearl he jerked back his head in surprise and said, "You are very honoured to have been given a pearl by Blue Fish. You must have proved you are worthy to be her friends. Any friend of Blue Fish is a friend of mine and will have my protection."

"You are lucky to have met Blue Fish ... and me. Without us you stand no chance of ever returning home. Voran or Spider, or one of their relatives, will kill and eat you and, if they don't, you'll die of hunger and thirst. That skull you found probably belonged to someone who got lost in these tunnels, and starved to death. Tomorrow I'll do you a favour and take you to the forest ... but tonight you must come with me and meet the others. If you sit on my tail, I'll take you to our den. Today is a special day; it's my cousin Verd's birthday."

With Thomas and Caitlin sitting on his tail, the red dragon lumbered further along the same tunnel until he came to a huge door made of tree trunks. He pushed it open and ushered them into a large warm well-lit cave. The floor was covered with rushes and, at one end, a fire blazed in an open hearth. In the middle of the cave stood a big wooden table heaped with food. There were jugs filled with cider, huge loaves of bread, an enormous bowl filled with hot steaming mushroom soup, heaps of apples, pears and chestnuts and whole sides of roast venison. Round this table, eight dragons of various shades of green, red and brown were seated.

When the red dragon entered, all the dragons stopped talking and stared in amazement. As Thomas and Caitlin walked towards the table, all eyes followed them. The silence was uncomfortable.

A large green dragon broke the silence. "Russ, have you gone mad, bringing young humans here ... especially on my birthday? Humans are our enemies and even young ones are not to be trusted." The others nodded and murmured in agreement.

In a flat tone Russ said, "Don't worry Verd, Blue Fish sent them."

An astonished gasp came from the assembled dragons.

"How do you know?" queried Verd.

Caitlin was worried. If they didn't believe it, she and Thomas might be imprisoned or even killed. She knew what to do. She held up Blue Fish's pearl for all to see. The dragons sat in silence and stared at the pearl, as if mesmerised by it. Immediately their attitude changed.

"I must apologise for our rudeness," said Verd. "Friends of Blue Fish are always welcome here."

"Welcome, welcome!" all the dragons shouted. "Sit down and eat."

"Wait," said Russ. "You are both tattered and dirty. Before you eat, you must wash and put on some clean clothes. I'll show you our bath."

He led them back along the passage to another chamber. From its doorway billowed warm air and steam. Inside was a pool of warm water, the size of a swimming pool, fed by hot water issuing from a big pipe sticking out of the rock.

"Where do you get the hot water from?" asked Caitlin.

"A pipe takes water from the underground river and passes through the side of the lava chamber where it gets heated."

"Clever!" commented Thomas.

Thomas and Caitlin undressed and were about to get into the water when Caitlin realised it was very deep.

"It's too deep for us to stand up in."

"Don't worry," said Russ. He slid into the pool, almost filling it, and lay on his back.

"If you sit on me, you'll be safe enough."

After their bath, Russ went to the dragons' nursery and came back with clothes made for baby dragons. They were brightly coloured ... in red, green and brown ... the same colours as the dragons themselves, and of strange designs, but they fitted reasonably well and were clean and comfortable.

They returned to the party. Dragons' chairs were much too big for Thomas and Caitlin so they sat on top of the table with their backs resting against one of the loaves. The dragons gave them portions of everything. It was the best food they had eaten since they left home and they ate heartily.

When the meal was finished, Verd's wife Greenie went to the kitchen and returned with a massive birthday cake - completely green, of course. On the top were three large candles, two medium-sized ones and five smaller ones. The candles were lit, and the dragons sang 'Happy Birthday.' Thomas and Caitlin could hear two versions at the same time. The one in their heads had words they could understand, but the other, from their ears, was just a lot of tuneless moaning and groaning. Verd blew out the candles with what he considered to be a gentle puff but, to Thomas and Caitlin, it seemed more like a hurricane. Slices of cake were passed round. The pieces given to Thomas and Caitlin were just as big as those given to the dragons and were about the same size as themselves. Being too polite to tell the dragons the slices were too big, they simply ate as much as they could. The cake was delicious, especially the thick cream in its centre.

Having eaten the cake, the dragons decided to play a game. They turned a broom upside down and placed it against the wall at one end of the cave. Standing at the other end, they took it in turns to breathe fire. The first to set the broom on fire would win a prize. Because it was his birthday, Verd was allowed to go first. A huge jet of flame shot the length of the room but did not quite reach the broom.

"Hard luck, Verd!" they shouted.

Brun was next, but his flame travelled only just over halfway. The others jeered and laughed. Three others tried, but none of their flames travelled the full distance. Russ took his turn. His flame reached the broom but was not powerful enough to set it on fire. Finally, Brownie stepped forward. He took a deep breath and, with a tremendous roar, expelled a huge flame which engulfed the broom and caused it to burst into flames. The dragons thumped their tails on the floor, clapped their wings together and cheered. Russ presented Brownie with the prize: a huge pot of beeswax. Dragons use it for polishing their scales.

Then it was time for some music. One of the dragons beat a large drum with its tail, another plucked the strings of a sort of harp with its claws, while yet another made a noise they supposed was meant to be singing. To Thomas and Caitlin it sounded terrible, but the dragons seemed to like it because they started to dance. The table shook, the ground trembled and the vibration caused scores of small pieces of rock to fall from the walls and roof of the cave. Thomas and Caitlin were worried they might get injured so, for safety, they dropped down onto the floor and sheltered beneath the table.

Later, when the party had finished, Russ said to them, "Now, tell everyone about yourselves and how you came to be here."

Thomas and Caitlin stood together in the centre of the table and took it in turns to tell the dragons the whole story. When they got to the part about Voran and Spider the dragons nodded in sympathy and, when they told of their escape, several of them shouted 'bravo!'

Then Russ said, "You've told us your story. Now I'll tell you ours, and how we came to live in these caves."

Chapter 11

The Dragons' Story

Russ sat back in one of the big chairs and began to tell the story:

"Hundreds of years ago, in the days when Arthur was king, and for many years afterwards, humans and dragons lived close by one another without there ever being any trouble. In fact, we often helped each other. If a farmer wanted a tree trunk lifting or a big stone moving, one of us would do it. In return, the farmer gave us some hay or did something we could not easily do ourselves ... such as make a table. Humans cultivated the open fields and dragons lived in the forest, which was then big enough to provide us with all the food we needed. However, as time passed, the humans wanted more farmland and started to cut down the trees.

"At first, because the forest was so big, we didn't worry but as it became smaller and smaller we became concerned. Even when humans had enough land to grow all the food they needed, they continued to fell the trees because some of them became greedy, and wanted to make themselves rich by selling the cleared land. We knew that if the forest became too small we would not have enough food to eat. So we pleaded with them to stop cutting down the trees. They took no notice.

"One day we happened to meet Earl Caradoc when he was riding in the forest. He was an ancestor of the present earl. I complained about the woodcutters and asked him for help. He appeared sympathetic and said, 'I'll try to persuade the woodcutters to leave the forest, but I must tell you I cannot order them to do so because the forest is common land and is for everyone's use.'

"Weeks passed and the woodcutters continued to cut down trees, with the result that a war between dragons and humans broke out."

Caitlin interrupted him. "You said all this happened hundreds of years ago, but you tell the story as if you had been there."

"Well ... I was there and I remember the events well."

"But it's too long ago."

"Not for us. Unlike humans, who live only a few years, we dragons live for hundreds of years. In fact, today is Verd's three hundred and twenty fifth birthday. Didn't you count the candles on the cake?"

"Three hundred and twenty-five!" repeated Thomas. "My grandad is sixty and we think he's old."

"Sixty years is nothing for a dragon," said Russ, and he continued the story.

"Each autumn we used to gather chestnuts and store them for use as food during the winter. On the day we arrived at the grove, we found the woodcutters had already cut down several chestnut trees.

"I spoke to Sab, the chief woodcutter. 'We need those chestnuts for food in the winter. Please don't cut down any more trees.'

"Sab shrugged his shoulders. 'Too bad! Our job is to clear the trees so the land can be used for farming.'

"'Didn't Earl Caradoc ask you to stop?' I asked.

"'No, he didn't. Anyway, what's it got to do with the Earl? The forest doesn't belong to him. In fact, it doesn't belong to anybody. We've every right to cut down the trees and claim the land. We are poor men; we need this land,' he said.

"'You already have enough land. Why d'you want more?' I retorted. 'Soon the forest will be too small to feed us and we'll starve.'

"We argued with him for a long time but he wouldn't listen.

"That night we held a meeting to discuss what to do. We decided to send Ochren to Caerdraig (which was then called Caercaradoc) to see the Earl. As you know, Caerdraig stands on the top of a long steep hill. With its many towers and massive walls of grey stone topped by battlements, it looked just as grim as it does today. Panting and puffing, Ochren slowly made his way up the stony track to its gates. As he crossed the drawbridge over the castle's moat, it creaked and groaned under his weight. The moat was much deeper than it is now and was filled with pointed stakes to stop horses being ridden across it. The guards watched his approach and, as he reached the iron-studded gates, the sergeant challenged him.

'Halt! Declare your business.'

'I wish to see the Earl,' said Ochren.

'What about?'

'The woodcutters felling the forest trees.'

The sergeant grimaced and said, 'The Earl's been expecting one of you to come up here,' and gave the order for Ochren to be admitted."

"Clattering noisily, the huge gates slowly swung back while the rising portcullis scraped and screeched against the stone walls of the gatehouse. Ochren passed under fearsome gargoyles, scowling

110

at him from high above the gateway, and entered the courtyard where a scene of great activity was revealed. A great many men were at work constructing two large wooden machines. Some were carrying long heavy timbers and others coils of thick rope. The courtyard rang to the sound of blacksmiths' hammers as they beat red-hot pieces of iron into bolts and other parts for the machines.

"A servant came out to meet Ochren. 'Wait here while I tell the Earl of your arrival,' he said.

"While he waited, Ochren watched the carpenters fastening timbers together.

"'What are you making?' he asked. They ignored his question.

"Again he asked but got no reply until a soldier standing nearby said, 'Earl Caradoc is going to fight the Saxons. These war machines are being made ready for battle.' At that moment the servant returned.

"'Follow me,' he said.

As they followed the servant to the Great Hall, one of the soldiers shouted, 'And the best of luck!' The others laughed. This made Ochren feel uneasy."

"Through big doors they entered one end of the Great Hall. Inside it was cold and gloomy, the only light coming from narrow slit-windows that had no glass in them. The floor was paved with large slabs of grey stone and, except for some tapestries hung on them, the stone walls were bare The tapestries depicted scenes of battle. One of them showed the Earl, with his sword raised, about to kill one of his foes.

"At the far end of the hall the Earl sat in a huge black chair, its arms and legs shaped like those of a lion, its back topped by the carved head of an eagle. Dressed in chain mail covered by a pale grey tabard sporting a picture of a golden griffin, he sat bolt upright. His arms rested on the arms of the chair with his hands gripping the clawed ends. By his side, dressed in an ankle-length, high-necked, dark red dress, stood a beautiful, tall and slim young woman whose long, flowing black hair cascaded onto her shoulders. On a chain she held a large fierce-looking grey dog, which growled menacingly as Ochren approached.

"Ochren stopped before the Earl and made his complaint. While he listened, the Earl fixed his piercing grey eyes on Ochren and neither smiled nor frowned. The tall young woman was also impassive and said nothing.

"Then the Earl said, 'Sab has told you the truth about the forest. It is common land. I tried to persuade him not to cut down any more trees, but he wouldn't agree.'

"Ochren said, 'Why didn't you order him to stop?'

"'I cannot order him to stop; I can only ask.'

"Ochren wasn't convinced. 'You are a powerful man, with much wealth and many soldiers. I think you can stop him if you want.'

"'There's nothing lawful I can do. If I send soldiers to stop him, he'll complain to the king.'

"Ochren was distressed. 'If he continues to cut down the trees we will starve. Is that what you want?'

"The Earl shrugged his shoulders. 'Of course I don't want you to starve. Like you, I don't want the forest cleared. I'll try once again to get him to stop.'

"Ochren didn't know whether to believe the Earl and hurriedly left the castle."

"Our plea to the Earl proved useless. All through the winter the woodcutters continued their work and by the following spring they had cut down hundreds of trees. We had to act. To protect the remaining forest from the woodcutters, we decided to construct a high fence made out of tree trunks.

"While we were building it, Sab came up to us and said angrily, 'What do you think you're doing? You cannot fence off the forest like this.'

"'You said the forest belongs to everybody,' I replied. 'If you can claim parts of it then so can we.' Sab was angry and shouted, 'We'll see about that!'"

"Soon afterwards, the woodcutters retaliated by bringing along a battering ram which they used to

knock down part of the fence. This made my
brother Brun very angry. He breathed fire over the
battering ram and set it alight. The woodcutters took
fright and ran off. A few days went by when
nothing happened and we continued to build the
fence. We thought we had scared them off for good
... but we were wrong."

Chapter 12

Battle in the Forest

"A few days later there was a battle. I'll tell you about it.

"We'd been hard at work all morning and had sat down to have a rest and a drink. Brun suddenly stood up. He pointed towards the castle and said, 'Listen. Can you hear that noise?'

"We sat in silence, listening intently, wondering what was making the noise. It was getting louder. Now we could hear what it was: the voices of scores of men, the sound of tramping feet, the snorts of horses and the rumble of cart wheels. Led by a company of archers, we saw dozens of soldiers coming, some on foot and some on horseback.

"Ochren gasped when he saw them and said, 'Those are the Earl's soldiers, the same ones I saw when I visited the castle.'

"Behind the archers and the soldiers, teams of horses were pulling huge siege catapults and cartloads of big rocks.

"'I saw those catapults being made,' said Ochren. 'The soldiers said they were for war on the Saxons. They lied. We've been tricked.'

"A sergeant shouted, 'Halt!' They'd spotted us.

"The Earl rode up on his horse and said, 'Pull down the fence and leave this area right now, or it will be the worse for you.'

"Brun was defiant. 'Whatever you do we will not remove our fence!' We all cheered.

"'Very well,' said the Earl. He signalled to the archers.

"They had already formed a long line in front of the rest of the soldiers, and each had an arrow in his bow ready to fire.

"'Fire!' shouted their leader.

"A hail of arrows flew high into the air … whooooo … and came down on us. Thud, thud, thud … Brun and Maron were hit, several arrows stuck in their backs. Blood gushed from the wounds. Roaring and breathing fire, we charged the archers. Some archers, their clothes on fire, ran away. Others, we struck down with our tails and trampled on them The rest stepped back and prepared to fire another volley of arrows.

"Scarlet started running. As he went, he shouted, 'I'll get the others.'

"We were outnumbered, but kept fighting because we thought we might yet win. Soon, the others arrived but were met by another hail of arrows. Many were wounded. Despite the pain from arrows sticking in our bodies we continued to charge the archers. However, behind the archers and the soldiers, we saw the catapults being made ready. Now, huge stones were flung at us. Two dragons were struck down and lay injured on the ground. Yet more stones were fired. We couldn't advance any further. Then, holding long spears in front of them, the soldiers advanced on us. They stabbed us repeatedly, forcing us to retreat."

Caitlin asked, "Was that the end of the battle?"

"Yes... but the start of a long war between us and the Earl."

"A few days later, Ochren went to see how many more trees had been cut down. He didn't return that day or the next. Two of us went to find him ... which we did. He was lying at the bottom of a huge pit ... dead ... impaled on sharp wooden stakes. The soldiers had laid a trap. They'd dug a pit and covered it with thin branches, grass and leaves so that it looked just like the rest of the ground. Ochren had stepped on the covering and fallen through into the pit."

"What a terrible thing to do!" cried Caitlin.

"After that we were very careful where we walked but, despite our care, occasionally a dragon would fall into one of the traps."

"So, those are the bones in the pit," said Caitlin.

"Sadly, yes."

Thomas asked, "How many died?"

"Four of us." A few tears trickled down Russ's cheeks.

He was silent for a few seconds while he composed himself.

"Before we lost the war with the Earl, we lived in caves in the side of a ravine hidden in the deepest part of the forest. It was difficult to find the ravine because brambles, bushes, tall trees, and masses of creepers surrounded it and hid it from view. Flowing along the floor of the ravine is a river which eventually goes underground, the same river in which you nearly drowned. Earl Caradoc wasn't satisfied he had defeated us in battle, he wanted to find out where we lived so he could destroy our homes and drive us from the forest.

"He ordered his men to capture one of us. We knew about the pit traps and were on the lookout for them, but we didn't know the Earl's men had invented a new type of trap; a large net laid on the ground and covered with leaves. Umber was caught in one. Struggle as he might, he couldn't free himself. Soldiers, hiding nearby, soon found him. They put chains round his body and shackles on his legs, all the time prodding him with the sharp points of their spears."

"But didn't he breathe fire over them?" queried Thomas.

"Yes he did but, between puffs, they tied a rope round his jaws. Using horses, they dragged him onto a cart and took him to the castle where he was chained by his legs to four massive iron stakes set up in the courtyard."

"As soon as the chains were secure, the Earl came out and walked right round him, marvelling at his enormous size. He said to Umber, 'I've captured you because I want you to take me to your village.'

"'Why do you want me to take you there?' asked Umber.

"'I want to meet all the dragons and make peace with them,' replied the Earl.

"'I don't believe you. You are full of lies, like the lies you told us about the woodcutters,' shouted Umber.

"'This time I'm telling the truth,' said the Earl.

"'I still don't believe you. The answer is no!' snapped Umber."

"The Earl shrugged his shoulders and walked away. Each day he came back, asked the same question and received the same reply."

"On the fifth day, the Earl said, 'I only want you to help me end the war. It will be good for everyone. If the war continues, I cannot say what will become of you all.'

"'I'm not going to help you!' shouted Umber. 'You are a liar and a murderer and are not to be trusted.'

"Angered by Umber's words, the Earl turned on his heels and strode off back to the Great Hall."

"Later that day he returned and ordered his soldiers to take Umber up to the battlements. With difficulty, using ropes, pulleys and teams of horses, they hauled him up a ramp and onto the gatehouse roof.

"Pointing across the remaining forest, the Earl said, 'I am a generous man. I'm prepared to give each dragon family a portion of the forest to live in. Your fellow dragons will be happy to own a piece of forest and will be pleased with you for helping end the war. What do you think of my offer?' Umber snorted and did not reply.

"The Earl looked thoughtfully at Umber and said, 'As a reward for your help, I'll give your family double the amount of land. Do you see that part of the forest over there, just beyond the giant oak tree? It will be reserved just for you and your family, and I'll send my soldiers to protect you.'

"Umber was enraged by this attempt to bribe him. 'You're wasting your breath. We dragons have lived in this forest for hundreds of years and we know it isn't yours. We'll fight to the death rather than let you destroy it.' He breathed fire at the Earl causing him to jump out of the way."

"Two days later, Morah, the beautiful young woman Ochren had seen in the Great Hall, came to see Umber.

"She spoke to him in a soft pleasant voice and said, 'You know, the Earl is being very generous offering you the best part of the forest to live in.'

"Umber said, "I don't trust him. It's a trick.'

"Morah said, 'I know Earl Caradoc well. He's not a bad man, he just wants the best for everyone.'

"'If he's not a bad man,' said Umber, 'why has he killed my relatives and destroyed part of the forest? And why is he holding me prisoner?'

"'He had to capture one of you because he knew the dragons wouldn't listen to him unless one of you was with him,' said Morah. Umber was not convinced but was in no mood to argue because he felt hungry and thirsty.

"'Why is the Earl starving me? I've not been given anything to eat or drink since yesterday morning,' he complained.

"Morah pretended to be surprised. 'Oh, I didn't know that. I'm quite sure he didn't tell his servants to neglect you. The servant responsible must simply have forgotten to feed you.' She smiled sweetly and stroked his neck with her smooth warm hands. The lovely odour of her perfume reached his nostrils. It was intoxicating and made him feel a little dizzy.

"In a sweet and gentle voice she said, 'You poor dragon, I'll bring you some food but, after your ordeal, you deserve something better than water to drink.'

"She went to the kitchens and came back carrying a large bowl and a jug, accompanied by a servant wheeling a cart containing five loaves of bread and a whole cheese.

"When Umber had eaten the bread and cheese, Morah said, 'This jug contains a drink made from honey and the juiciest purple plums I could find. It tastes delicious and I think you'll like it.' She poured a little into a glass and sipped it.

"'Yes,' she said, nodding her head, 'it's as good as when I first made it.'

"She poured the rest into the bowl and offered it to Umber. Umber was a bit suspicious but, having seen Morah drink some, thought it must be safe. Lowering his head, he dipped his tongue in it. It really was delicious. He began to drink and the more he drank the more he wanted to drink. Very soon he had drunk it all."

"Shortly afterwards, the Earl entered the courtyard. Morah greeted him with a kiss and whispered in his ear. He turned his attention to Umber.

"'Morah tells me my servant forgot to feed you. I'm sorry about that. I'll have him punished.'

"Again, he made the same offer. 'Have you thought about what I said the other day? Just think, we could all live together in peace and you would be a hero among the dragons for having made peace with me.'"

"Umber now began to think the Earl wasn't really such a bad man and was sincere in wanting to make peace. *'Perhaps his offer of parts of the forest for each dragon family was really quite generous. After all, the Earl's soldiers did control most of the forest …'* and the thought of being a hero appealed to him.

"He said, 'Well ... you've won the war so I suppose it's time for us to make peace. I'll take you to meet my kin ... but on one condition.'

"The smile that had formed on the Earl's face faded. 'What condition?'

"'No soldiers are to come with us.'

"The smile returned. 'That's no problem. Let's not waste any more time. We must set off at once.'"

"With Earl Caradoc on horseback, and two of his servants on foot, they set off for our village. Some way behind, moving very quietly, a troop of heavily armed soldiers followed. Late in the afternoon, as they neared the ravine, they passed the statue of Goch, founder of our village. Scarlet, whose turn it was to act as sentry, met them.

"He challenged Umber. 'Where've you been this past week, and why have you brought Earl Caradoc with you? He's our enemy.'

"Umber replied, 'The Earl wants to end the war. He wants to make peace with us.'

"'That's right', said the Earl. 'If we make peace I'll give each of your families parts of the forest to live in.'

"'The forest isn't yours to give!' snapped Scarlet.

"'Oh, yes it is,' said the Earl.

"'No, it's not!' shouted Scarlet.

"Umber said, 'Why don't we hear what the Earl is going to give us?'

"'It isn't his to give!' retorted Scarlet angrily.

"'Well, his soldiers control most of it,' reasoned Umber.

"'Whose side are you on, you traitor?' shouted Scarlet.

"'I'm not a traitor,' screamed Umber angrily. He breathed fire at Scarlet."

"Jumping back to avoid the flames, Scarlet retaliated. The flames scorched Umber's side. Slowly the two fire-breathing dragons circled each other, lashing out with their tails. Their roars filled the air and the ground shook. Rearing up on his hind legs, Umber attacked Scarlet, biting him on the shoulder and making deep blood-filled scratches on his back. Scarlet clawed Umber's head. Scratching and biting and covered in blood, the two of them went round and round, bumping against the surrounding trees causing them to lean over and making branches fall. Quite suddenly, struck by a heavy branch, Umber collapsed on the ground. Scarlet stopped, stared at Umber's prone figure, turned his head towards the Earl and emitted an enormous jet of flame. Terrified, the Earl whipped his horse to a gallop and fled.

"I turned to a young dragon standing nearby and said, 'Fly to Emrys's cottage and ask for his help.'"

"Was Umber badly hurt? Did he die?" queried Caitlin.

"Emrys examined Umber and said, 'He's lost a lot of blood and is unconscious, but I don't think he'll die. When I've treated his wounds you must take him home and let him rest until he's better.'

"We carried Umber back to his cave in the ravine and looked after him. He was very weak from loss of blood but, after several weeks, he recovered."

"Oh, I'm glad he was alright," said Caitlin.

"And so am I," said someone on the far side of the cave. They looked across to where a pale brown dragon was standing.

Russ said, "That's Umber."

Chapter 13

Riddle Solved

Russ continued the story.

"Some weeks later, we saw a man bearing a large white flag come riding through the trees. He was a messenger, sent by the Earl to negotiate with us.

"'Earl Caradoc sends you his greetings,' he said. 'He has sent me to offer you an honourable way out of your sorry plight, one for which you have only yourselves to blame.' There were angry shouts when he said this.

"Struggling to make himself heard, the messenger continued, 'As the Earl is a kind and generous man ...' More angry shouting interrupted him. '... and despite your stubbornness ... he is still prepared to set aside part of the forest for you to live in.'

"There was uproar. Verd shouted, 'Kind and generous, kind and generous. He's not kind and generous. He's a cruel and heartless thief!'

"'And a murderer,' several shouted.

"The messenger turned pale with fright but did not run away. 'Remember, I'm only the messenger,' he pleaded.

"With shaking hands, he pulled a map out of his bag and unrolled it. It showed the area of forest the Earl would allow us to live in.

"I looked at it and said, 'That area is far too small to provide us with the food we need. How will we survive?'

"The messenger said, 'As I have already told you, the Earl is kind and generous. He will give you the extra food you need.' He paused, swallowed hard and said, '... provided you work for it.'

"'Work for it!' spluttered Brun. 'Does he think we'd agree to that? If we did, we'd be his slaves.' Everyone agreed with Brun. The messenger trembled with fear.

"I said to him, 'Go back to the castle and tell your master he is a murderer and a thief and that we'll never give up the struggle.' The messenger jumped on his horse and rode off."

Choking back his tears, Russ carried on telling the story.

"The battles with the Earl's men went on for years but, little by little, we lost control of the whole forest. Our flames and claws were no match for their siege catapults, arrows, swords, spears and suits of armour. One day, the Earl's men found our village and burned our homes. We retreated into the old mine tunnels and lived in underground caves, where we still live. To celebrate their victory, the Earl's soldiers dragged the statue of Goch to the castle and stood it by the gates, where it still stands to this day."

"Was that the end of the war?" queried Thomas. "Has anything happened since?"

"It was the end of the war but it's not the end of the story."

"Now, around this time, a soldier had a cunning idea. He said to the Earl, 'If we can capture some of the small dragons, we can put them in cages and sell them to a travelling circus or a showman. That'll get rid of them and make you some money.'

"Earl Caradoc said, 'That's a good idea. You must work out how to do it.'

"He beckoned to a nearby servant and said, 'Tell the bursar to give this man two gold pieces now and two more when he has captured a small dragon.'

"The soldiers laid net traps all over the forest. Soon they captured my daughter Rosa, imprisoned her in a large cage and sold her. I've not seen her since." Tears rolled down his cheeks.

Caitlin was puzzled. "Why is there so much forest left today? Did the Earl change his mind about clearing it?"

"Fortunately for us, less of the forest was cleared than the Earl had planned. While out riding in the forest one day, his horse stumbled and threw him. He fell into one of his own traps and a stake went through his heart."

"Good!" shouted Thomas. "He deserved to die like that."

Russ agreed and carried on with the story.

"His son took over his father's estate and, because he liked to hunt deer and wild boar, he decided the remaining forest should be preserved. The felling of trees ceased. However, we were still unable to live in the forest because the new Earl knew we were taking deer and wild boar for food. To try to stop us, he sent his men to patrol the forest during the day. Even now, we only go into the forest at dawn and dusk. As a result, we aren't able to gather much food. That's why we sometimes steal farmers' crops and animals. If we didn't, we would starve."

Thomas had a question. "You all have wings. Why didn't you just fly to another valley?"

"We tried to do that but we are not strong fliers and the mountains round this valley are too high for us to cross. We long for the day when we can live openly in the forest once more, but that will never happen unless the present Earl allows it."

"How do you know he won't allow it?" asked Caitlin.

"I suppose we don't," admitted Russ. "We've never met him."

Caitlin wanted to know about Voran, Spider and Blue Fish.

"Voran and Spider tried to kill and eat us. Where did they come from?"

"They lived in the caves before we did. Sometimes they ate our babies so they became our enemies."

"What about Blue Fish? Was she already there?"

"Blue Fish is different. The reason for her presence is a secret which I cannot tell you. For now, she will have to remain a mystery to you. She is very powerful. All who live in these caves and tunnels know of her power and have great respect for her."

"Even Voran and Spider?" asked Thomas.

"They are enemies of Blue Fish but they're also afraid of her," replied Russ.

Thomas and Caitlin were puzzled. *'How could a fish be so powerful?'*

Thomas wanted to know how many dragons lived in the caves.

"The nine adults you see here plus our children."

Caitlin looked at the nine dragons and suddenly realised she had the answer to the riddle, and understood what Blue Fish had meant when she said their mission would become clear to them.

"Nine!" she exclaimed. The dragons stared at her, wondering what was so special about the number nine.

She whispered to Thomas, "I know what Blue Fish's riddle means."

"What?"

"Look carefully at the dragons and think about it." She repeated the riddle:

"When three times three
Are like the leaves of a tree
Then a favour granted
Must be repaid."

Thomas looked at the dragons and said, "I understand the 'three times three' bit but not the rest."

"Look at their colours."

With a quizzical look on his face, he looked at them carefully.

"I still don't understand."

Putting her mouth close to his ear, Caitlin whispered the answer. Immediately his face lit up.

"Oh, now I understand," he said.

Caitlin explained. "They are going to do us a favour by taking us to the surface. So we must repay them."

"How can we do that?" asked Thomas.

"When we get back home, we must tell Mum and Dad the dragons' story, and ask them to go with us to persuade the Earl to let the dragons live in the forest again."

Russ heard what Caitlin said and thanked her. He added, "If you succeed, we'll be able to go back to the old village, but we won't entirely forsake our underground homes."

"Why not?" asked Thomas.

"Because we are allies of Blue Fish, and have to help her guard the underground lake."

"Why does it need guarding?" asked Caitlin.

"I can't tell you ... but no more questions. It's time for you to rest."

He led them to a small cave off one side of the dining chamber. In it were two big heaps of hay.

"If you snuggle down in the hay I think you will sleep well," he said.

For the first time since they had entered the caves they felt safe. Warm and well-fed, they soon fell asleep.

Chapter 14

The Forest of Terror

Next day, as promised, Russ made preparations for the journey to the surface. He decided he would carry Thomas and Caitlin on his back and would be guarded by Verd and Brun.

"Climb on my back and hold tight to the base of my wings," he said. "The journey might be dangerous because it takes us through territory belonging to Voran's family. But don't worry, we'll guard you well."

Using the dragon's knee as a step, Thomas and Caitlin climbed up and sat side by side between his wings. With Verd, the large green dragon, travelling in front and Brun behind, they set off. Because the dragons were so big, they were only able to walk through tunnels which they had specially enlarged. As a result, the journey was long and winding, with many turns. Down tunnel after tunnel and through cave after cave they went, none of which Thomas and Caitlin recognised. They remembered what Russ had told them: if they hadn't met Blue Fish and himself they wouldn't have stood a chance of escaping. Now they knew it was true.

Occasionally, in order to see more clearly where they were going, Verd breathed fire. Once, they saw the white animal Thomas had previously seen, standing staring at them. It was a wolf.

After travelling for several hours, occasionally stopping to rest, they entered an unusually wide tunnel. Now the dragons walked very slowly.

"Why are we going so slowly?" asked Thomas.

"Hush!" said Verd in a low voice. "We are entering Voran's territory so we must move as quietly as we can."

Taking one carefully placed step at a time, they advanced. A few yards ahead they heard some small stones falling from the roof of the tunnel. This often happened but, this time, the dragons were suspicious and stopped. Verd breathed fire and looked and listened. Nothing unusual could be seen or heard. They moved on a couple of steps, stopped and listened again ... nothing. Another two steps ... blood-curdling shrieks pierced the silence.

Amidst a huge shower of stones, two monsters, almost identical to Voran in appearance, dropped down from the roof, a black one in front and a grey one behind. Thomas and Caitlin's hearts raced. Verd breathed fire over the black one. It backed away ... but the grey one jumped onto Brun's back and wrapped its tail round his throat. Brun coughed and choked and shouted to Russ for help. At that same moment, Voran himself emerged from a crevice in the wall of the tunnel and sprang onto Russ's back. He tried to seize Caitlin's legs in his jaws but she kicked at his head with all her strength. Holding on tight to Russ's wings, Thomas joined in the kicking, causing Voran to lose his grip and fall to the ground. Russ wasted no time, he stamped on Voran scratching him with his huge claws. Bruised and bleeding, Voran staggered to his feet and limped off into the darkness.

Brun, still with Grey Voran's tail wrapped round his throat, was now on his knees, gradually losing consciousness. Russ went to his aid. He sank his teeth into Grey Voran's tail. Screaming with pain, Grey Voran released his grip on Brun's throat, jumped down from Brun's back and charged Russ, trying to skewer him with his horn ... but Russ was too quick and dodged out of the way. Grey Voran struck the wall of the tunnel heavily and collapsed unconscious on the ground. Seeing his friend collapse, Black Voran gave up trying to attack Verd, bellowed, turned tail and ran off.

Thomas was exultant. He stood up and waved his arms in the air. "We've beaten them. We've beaten them!" he shouted.

"Will they come back?" asked Caitlin.

"No," said Russ, "they've had enough for now."

The dragons examined one another's wounds. Having decided that no-one was seriously injured, they continued their journey.

After another mile, the tunnel started to rise steeply. A series of shallow steps cut into its floor were seen.

Caitlin was excited. "Look Thomas, we're heading for those steps. We must be nearly there."

The dragons struggled up the steps and stopped on a broad landing. In front of them was the end of the tunnel ... a blank wall. There seemed to be no way out.

Thomas was puzzled. "Have we gone the wrong way?"

"Look up," said Russ.

Above them, set in the tunnel roof was a pair of large wooden shutters.

"We've reached the surface," said Russ.

The dragons pressed their backs against the shutters, pushing with all their might. Slowly the shutters opened and fell back. Thomas and Caitlin stepped off Russ's back onto the ground above.

"We're free, we're free!" shouted Thomas while Caitlin wept with joy.

The air was cold but smelt fresh. They took deep breaths. It was so much better than the dank air of the tunnels.

"Isn't it great to be out in the open again?" said Caitlin.

"Oh yes. I thought we'd never escape," said Thomas.

Caitlin turned to Russ. "Thank you for bringing us here. You were right; without your help, we'd never have reached the surface ... would we, Thomas?"

"No, we wouldn't. We won't forget you. When we get back home we'll keep our promise. We'll ask the Earl to let you live in the forest once more."

Caitlin looked round at the dark forest and was worried.

"Russ, will we be safe? There are bears and wolves in the forest. They might kill us. Please can one of you come with us?"

"There's no need to be afraid," he said. "All the animals in the forest, even the bears and wolves, know about Blue Fish. If you show them the pearl you'll be safe."

"But we don't know where we are," protested Thomas.

"Don't worry, you'll find your way back home. I know for sure you will."

Russ handed him one of his red scales, one loosened during the fight.

"After you arrive home, leave this scale by the river entrance to let us know you are safe."

The dragons said goodbye and descended into the tunnel. Russ was last to go. With a final shout "Goodbye and good luck!" he pulled the shutters closed.

Suddenly they felt very alone, abandoned at the dead of night somewhere deep in the heart of a vast dark forest which had a terrifying reputation. They did not know whereabouts in the forest they were, but realised they were nowhere near its edge. This entrance was hidden in a dense thicket of thorn bushes and brambles and was not the one by which they had first entered the tunnels.

It was cold and still. From high in the sky, the full moon shone through leafless trees, its light reflected from a sprinkling of snow covering the frozen ground. They remembered it had been summertime when they first entered the tunnels and now realised they must have been down in them for months ... or even longer. Shivering from the cold, they wondered which way to go. They tried first one way and then another but, whichever way they tried, they found it difficult to make any progress because the brambles seemed to be holding them prisoner. The long prickly stems hooked themselves onto their clothes, becoming more firmly attached with every move they made.

R ... i ... p. "Oh, my dress is torn," cried Caitlin.

"Ow!" cried Thomas. The brambles had made a long scratch on his arm. Tearing at their bare arms and legs they produced more sore bleeding scratches.

"Horrid brambles!" shouted Thomas. He picked up a stick, beat the brambles down and stamped on them. Caitlin copied. Little by little, they managed to make a path out into open ground. Escaping from the thicket, they left it behind.

Soon they were walking along a broad grassy path between tall pine trees. With each footstep the frost-encrusted grass crackled beneath their feet. Under the trees, where the moon didn't shine, it was very dark and, in that darkness, they heard rustling sounds and little snarls. They felt nervous. They sensed they were being watched ... by things in the dark waiting to pounce ... ready to bite ... and tear ... and kill ... and eat. Caitlin held onto Thomas's arm tightly with one hand and slid her other hand into her pouch to take hold of the pearl.

Trying not to make a sound they hurried on, but occasionally trod on a twig, which broke with a loud echoing snap. This made them even more fearful because they knew the things in the dark would hear the noise and know exactly where they were. Then those dreadful creatures might lie in wait, ready to pounce on them.

A shiver ran down Thomas's spine; he had the feeling something was following them. They glanced back and caught sight of many pairs of cruel-looking eyes glinting in the moonlight. Their hearts raced and thumped with fear. Caitlin started to cry. Her cries were copied by a chorus of hideous shrieks from the things in the dark. When she cried they shrieked, and when she was quiet so were they. To terrify them even more, the white wolf emerged from the shadows, stared at them with its pale piercing eyes, raised its head and howled, a long drawn-out howl which echoed back from far, far away. Thinking it might attack, they clung to one another but, as suddenly as it had appeared, it disappeared back into the shadows.

The path gradually narrowed, making the bushes and trees ... and the darkness beneath them ... close in. The awful screeches became louder and more menacing. They wanted to hide, to escape from the things in the dark, but there was nowhere to go. An owl swooped down from a nearby tree. On silent wings it flew low over their heads, staring at them with its big round eyes, before continuing on into the night.

Ahead of them, glowing in the moonlight, long wisps of mist, floating just above the ground, appeared among the trees. To their amazement, the wisps slowly drifting through the trees, wound themselves together merging to form a large luminous cloud. They were unable to take their eyes off the cloud and stood stock-still, staring at it. Slowly it moved towards them and gradually enveloped them.

Now everything changed. Inside the cloud they felt warm, at peace and no longer frightened. They were in a trance, as if they had been hypnotised. The cloud now moved off them and, at a leisurely pace, floated through the trees. They felt compelled to follow. It led them on and on through the forest. Through bushes, over bare ground, across frozen swampy areas and rushing streams, mile after mile it travelled. Everywhere it went, the things in the dark fell silent until it passed by.

Eventually they reached an old ruined church on the edge of the forest, just beyond the last of the trees. As they approached, an owl, sitting on top of the church tower, hooted with long wavering notes.

The bright moonlight revealed a graveyard filled with bushes, brambles and the long-dead grass of summer. The ghost, for that is what it was, wove a path through the tangled vegetation. Close to the church's ivy-covered south wall were some ancient gravestones. The ghost paused near one of them. Unravelling to form a long thin trail of mist once more, it slowly filtered into the ground. As it went, Thomas and Caitlin gradually came out of the trance. They were confused and had only a vague recollection of what had happened.

"How did we get here?" asked Caitlin.

"I'm not sure," answered Thomas, "but I think we walked into a cloud of mist ... and somehow arrived here."

The graveyard and the ruined church looked familiar.

It dawned on Thomas where they were. "I know this place, don't you?"

"Yes," replied Caitlin feeling elated. "It's the ruined church not far from our cottage. We'll soon be home."

A red glow was developing on the eastern horizon; it was beginning to get light. In the distance they could see their cottage. Smoke rising from its chimney showed their parents to be awake. As they made their way across the frosty fields, a golden eagle circled high in the sky several times before flying off towards the village. Lighter and lighter it became until, finally, the sun rose, a huge dazzling golden disc in a pure blue cloudless sky. Soon they would be home, safe from the monsters that dwelt in the dark, dank tunnels, safe from the savage things hidden in the forest.

When they were quite close to the cottage they saw their mother come out and go over to the well to draw water.

"Mum, Mum, we're back!" they shouted.

She stared but did not recognise them. That was not surprising because they were wearing very strange clothes, their faces were covered in dirt and they had greasy matted hair hanging down over their shoulders.

"Go away," she said. "It's no use coming here. We can't help you. We are too poor. Go to the village and ask the priest for alms. He always tries to help beggars."

Caitlin was dismayed by her reaction. "Mum, don't you recognise us? We're not beggars. We're your children."

The voice sounded familiar. She put down her bucket and stared. They came closer. Realising they really were her children, she was overjoyed.

Tears rolled down her face as she hugged and kissed them. "Thomas, Caitlin, where have you been?"

She summoned their father. "Evan ... Evan, Thomas and Caitlin have come back. Quick, come and see them!"

Evan hurried from the barn, but hesitated when he saw the two dirty little figures. For an instant he wondered if his wife was mistaken.

"Caitlin? Thomas?" he queried.

"Yes, Dad, it's us," replied Caitlin, running up to him and putting her arms round his waist. The sound of her voice convinced him. At long last, his children really had returned.

"Caitlin, Thomas, you're back. I can hardly believe it." He put his arms round them both and cuddled them closely.

"Where have you been all this time?" asked their mother. "I thought you were dead."

"So did I," added Evan.

"We went into the tunnels to look for silver and got lost," said Thomas. "Then we were captured by a monster who was going to eat us ... but I'm so hungry, please can I have something to eat?"

"Of course," replied Gwyn. With an arm round each of his children, Evan walked them into the cottage where Gwyn made some porridge.

When they had finished eating, Gwyn heated some water over the fire and poured it into a big wooden tub placed on the floor of the downstairs room. She cut their hair, washed them and gave them clean clothes. While being bathed, they told their parents all about their adventures. Gwyn and Evan listened and, although they were happy to have their children back again, they were cross with them for having put themselves in so much danger.

Gwyn said, "When you didn't come home we went round the village asking everybody if they knew where you were. Nobody did. Next day, when you still hadn't returned, we were very worried. The villagers helped us search, but there was no sign of you anywhere. We feared we might never see you again, that you had disappeared, just as Dafydd and Ioan did all those years ago. Each night we prayed for your return and the priest also prayed for you. Now God has answered our prayers. It's a miracle!" She knelt down and said a prayer of thanks.

Mention of Dafydd and Ioan reminded Caitlin of what they had seen.

In a quiet voice she said slowly, "We think we know what happened to Dafydd and Ioan. In the monster's cave we saw torn-up clothes and two small human skulls."

Gwyn was horrified. "Poor things. I'm so sorry for their parents. Just think, you too would have been eaten, had you not escaped."

Later that day, Thomas told his father about the promise they had given Russ.

"If we hadn't met Russ, we would never have escaped from the tunnels. The dragons want to be able to roam the forest once more. We've promised to help them."

Evan knew he owed the dragons a great deal. "We'll go to the castle together to talk to the Earl," he said. "He's a kind man, not at all like his greedy ancestors."

To show the dragons their gratitude, Evan went to the river entrance of the mine that evening and left two sacks of cabbages, together with the red scale that Russ had given Thomas. The following morning the cabbages had gone and another red scale had been placed next to the first one.

Chapter 15

A Favour Repaid

Next day they went to see Emrys.

He greeted them with a smile. "I heard you were safely back."

They wondered how he knew because nobody had visited their farm and their parents had not been down to the village.

Caitlin was about to ask when he said, "Tell me everything that happened to you."

Taking it in turns, they told him about Voran, Spider, Blue Fish and the dragons, but it was Blue Fish who really interested him. He asked a lot of questions about her.

Caitlin was suspicious. "Blue Fish told us that a magician gave her the power to communicate with humans. Are you that magician?"

Emrys looked embarrassed. "Well ... I suppose it's obvious. You've already seen and heard much so I'll tell you the whole story."

"In the days after the Roman Legions left Britain, when Arthur was king and Merlin his magician, Blue Fish lived in a lake surrounding the Island of Avalon and was a companion of the Lady of the Lake. King Arthur had a magic sword called Excalibur. When King Arthur lay dying, he ordered his knight Sir Bedivere to throw Excalibur into the lake. As it fell, a slender white hand emerged from the water, caught it and brandished it before drawing it below the surface. The hand belonged to the Lady of the Lake. Afterwards, six maidens dressed in flowing black robes came in a boat and carried the king's body across the lake to the island. Later, when the Saxons threatened Avalon, Merlin transported the king's body to Wales and hid it in a cave close to one containing the bodies of his knights".

"Are they the warriors we saw in the crystal grotto?" asked Thomas.

"Yes. The legends are true when they say that none of them are really dead but only sleeping, and that one day they will again be called to defend Britain from invaders, just as they defended her from the Saxons."

"But why is Blue Fish living in the lake near the grotto?" asked Caitlin.

"I was Merlin's apprentice. When Merlin was on his death bed, he made me promise to guard the grotto. I couldn't spend all my time underground so I persuaded Blue Fish to guard it for me. In return, I endowed her with magical powers and the ability to communicate with me."

Thomas wanted to know more. "Blue Fish knows her way through the tunnels. How is that possible?"

"The answer lies in the spell I wove when Blue Fish agreed to guard Arthur and his knights. You solved a riddle Blue Fish gave you, so perhaps you will be able to understand the spell.

"Earth, air and water too
White is gold and gold is blue
Arthur sleeps within his bower
Protect him well with all your power."

They listened carefully, then asked Emrys to repeat it.

Caitlin frowned. "I don't understand."

"Nor do I," said Thomas."

"Think about what you've seen," said Emrys.

Caitlin wanted to know about the dragons.

"Why are the dragons friends of Blue Fish?"

"Goch, founder of the dragons' village, was the famous red dragon who helped King Arthur by fighting and defeating the Saxons' fearsome white dragon."

They were astonished by what Emrys had told them and sat thinking about it. It made sense of so many puzzling events.

Eventually Caitlin said, "We promised the dragons we would try to persuade the Earl to allow them to live in the forest once more. Blue Fish made it our mission."

Emrys smiled. "The present Earl is a kind man. I'm sure he will allow the dragons to return to the forest."

A few days later, Thomas and Caitlin, accompanied by Evan and Emrys, set off to visit the Earl. The castle, perched on the top of its hill, looked as grim as ever. They tried to imagine what Ochren's visit must have been like, all those years ago. As they neared the castle they passed the statue of Goch the red dragon, the reason for the castle's name. The statue is still there today, huge and impressive, guarding the entrance of the now ruined castle. The dragon stands on three legs with the remaining leg held up in front, its clawed foot ready to strike. It has a snarl on its face, its long red tongue sticking out between rows of sharp teeth.

With its wings raised and its tail stretched out behind, it looks very fierce.

Caitlin said, "Russ told us how the statue was taken here."

She told the others the story.

When they reached the castle, they found the drawbridge down, the gates wide open and the portcullis raised. There were no soldiers on guard and no weapons of war in the courtyard. Except for a few horses, a cart and a carriage, the courtyard was empty. Wondering which way to go, they stood in the courtyard until one of the Earl's servants spotted them and came out.

"Hello, Emrys. What brings you here?"

"My young friends have just returned after being lost in the old silver mines. They were missing for months and were feared dead. They have a tale to tell which will interest the Earl."

"Wait here while I inform the Earl," he said.

When he came back, he ushered them into the Great Hall where the Earl was waiting. Unlike his ancestor, he was not dressed in armour but in tight-fitting fawn trousers, long leather boots and a buttoned-up dark green jacket.

"Welcome to Caerdraig," he said. "I hear you got lost in the old silver mines."

He pointed to a table on which the servant had deposited some cakes, fruit and ale. "Sit down and tell me all about your ordeal."

He listened to their story, raising his eyebrows whenever dragons were mentioned.

"I've often been told stories about dragons who were supposed to have lived in the forest long ago, but I didn't know they were true. Now I know those stories are true ... and that dragons still live there. I'm amazed. Provided they don't eat all the deer and wild boar, I think it will be possible for them to live in the forest. However, before I make a final decision, I must meet Russ."

"I'll send a messenger to Russ asking him to meet us at the river entrance tomorrow morning," said Emrys.

Happy with what they had accomplished, they went back to the village. On the way, they met a stranger. The unhappy look on the man's face matched his neglected appearance. His hair and beard were unkempt and greasy, his clothes torn and dirty.

"Good day," said Evan. "I've not seen you in these parts before."

"No," replied the ragged man. "I've come from Penfawr on the coast. Terrible things have happened, and I no longer have a home."

"Why is that?"

"One afternoon, twenty Viking longboats came over the Western Sea. Scores of warriors spilled from the boats and ransacked the abbey on the island called Ynys Gwrach (Island of the Witch), murdering all the monks. Then they came to our village, searching for food and treasure. They had no mercy. Shouting and screaming with fury, and wielding their battle-axes and swords, they killed anyone who tried to stop them. When they had finished looting, they burned our cottages and took the remaining men, women and children away to be sold as slaves."

"What a dreadful story! How did you manage to escape?"

"I hid down a well and luckily they didn't find me." His voice faltered.

When he had composed himself he continued. "It's not the first time they've raided villages on the coast, but the raids have gradually become more daring and this was the worst. We aren't warriors and cannot fight them, and we don't know who we can ask to defend us."

Emrys said, "I've heard of these Vikings from other travellers. Something must be done to stop their raids. If not, it won't be long before they sail up the river and attack our village."

Evan felt sorry for the ragged man and said, "The cottage next to the church is empty, I think the priest might let you stay there."

While Evan and the ragged man went to see the priest, Thomas and Caitlin walked with Emrys back to his cottage. After stopping for a drink of water, they continued on their way home but hadn't gone far when Caitlin remembered she had left her pouch containing the precious blue pearl at the cottage. They retraced their steps and, as they passed through the bushes bordering the path leading to his door, they heard Emrys chanting in a strange language.

"It sounds as though he's casting a spell," said Caitlin. "Let's hide in the bushes and watch what he's doing."

They crept forward and peered through the leaves. As usual, Emrys had made a small fire outside. While they watched, he sprinkled some black powder on it. There was a burst of bright red flame and a small cloud of black smoke rose into the air.

Emrys raised his arm, pointed a finger at it and shouted, "Aquila!"

From high in the sky a golden eagle appeared. It cried out with a mewing sound and circled. Then it descended, landed on Emrys's arm, folded its wings and nibbled his hair. Emrys stroked the eagle, tickled its neck and muttered something. The bird bent its head to listen. Straight away it flew off and headed for the forest. They watched it until it was too small to be seen.

Caitlin muttered to herself very quietly, "White is gold and gold is blue."

"That was amazing," whispered Thomas. "Where do you think it's gone?"

"I don't know, but I think he's sent it on an errand."

Not wanting Emrys to know they'd been watching, they crept back along the path and went home.

Shortly after sunrise next day, they all gathered by the mine entrance. A few minutes later a chariot, drawn by a lively chestnut horse, came along the track. Some way behind trundled a covered cart. When both had arrived, Earl Caradoc stepped down from the chariot.

"Good morning, Emrys. Will the dragon come today?"

"Yes, my lord."

Caradoc signalled to his servants. "Unload the cart and bring the hampers over here."

The servants struggled with two enormous wicker hampers filled with food of all kinds.

"I'll fetch Russ," said Emrys.

He disappeared inside the mine entrance. After several minutes, he emerged ... with Russ following. Scared by his enormous size and ferocious appearance, the Earl backed away.

Russ noticed. "Don't be afraid, I won't harm you," he said.

The Earl held his head with both hands and stared in amazement at the dragon.

Reassured he was safe, the Earl recited the little speech he had prepared:

"I am pleased you agreed to meet me today. Thomas and Caitlin have told me all about you and your fellow dragons, and how you rescued them when they were lost underground. Their family and the whole village are grateful to you for their return. I have also been told how badly you were treated by my ancestors. Times have changed and I promise such events will never happen again. Provided you do not eat too many forest animals, you are welcome to live in the forest once more."

Russ was happy. To show his happiness, but much to the consternation of everyone present, he blew flames high into the air.

Thanking the Earl, he said, "I speak on behalf of all the dragons when I say we are overjoyed to know we shall be able to live in the forest without fear of persecution. Thank you for your generosity. We shall look after the forest and its animals."

Russ bowed and the Earl saluted him. Climbing onto his chariot, the Earl urged the horse to a trot and set off back to the castle. Russ thanked the others for what they had done and retreated into the mine. The mission Blue Fish had given Thomas and Caitlin had been fulfilled and the favour granted truly repaid.

However ... not everyone was happy. A short distance away, hidden behind some trees, an ugly old woman was lurking. She had watched and listened, and wasn't pleased.

Months passed, summer came again. Since their terrible adventures, Thomas and Caitlin had not dared go anywhere near the mine. However, they often talked about all that had happened, and particularly about the cloud of mist.

"I don't think it was mist," said Caitlin. "I saw the last of it filtering into the ground by an old gravestone. I think it was a ghost."

"Well, if you're right, it must have been a friendly one, because it led us out of the forest," said Thomas. "I think we should go to the old graveyard again and find out who is buried there." They told their father what they were thinking.

Now, the old church had not been used for over a hundred years. After a new church was built in the village, people stopped using the old one. As time went by, the thatch blew off the roof and the timbers rotted away. In due course the roof collapsed, the weather eroded the stonework and parts of the walls fell down. Year by year it became more ruinous. Ivy grew over the tower and trees started to grow inside. Foxes and badgers made their homes in the crypt while owls nested in the tower. Scary stories began to circulate concerning the forest and the old church. These stories made their father reluctant to take them there but, after he had persuaded the priest to accompany them, he agreed to go.

One sunny afternoon they crossed the flower-spangled fields and arrived at the old churchyard. Winding their way through the bushes, brambles and long grass, they soon found the grave. It was instantly recognisable because it had a carving of the face of the Green Man on the gravestone: a round smiling face with leaves growing out of its ears and nostrils. The grave was clearly very old. Beneath the carving, there appeared to be an inscription, but it was hard to see because it was covered with moss. Evan scraped off the moss so the priest could read it. Translated into English, it read:

'Here lies the body
of
Gwilym of the Greenwood.
To the traveller lost in the forest
He was always a friend.
Gold had he not, save in his heart.
May the Lord guard his soul.'

They felt grateful to old Gwilym and asked the priest to say a prayer for him.

Chapter 16

The Horse Market

Each year, on a day in early June, a horse market was held in the village. People came to the market from miles around to buy and sell horses. With the horses came jugglers, fire-eaters, dancers, acrobats, musicians, sellers of food and, occasionally, strange animals. Thomas and Caitlin liked going to the horse market and particularly liked seeing the strange animals.

On the day of the market, chattering excitedly, they walked with their mother and father down the road to the village.

"I love horses," said Caitlin. "I'm going to look at them all and choose the one I like best."

Thomas wasn't interested in horses. "We see horses all the time; they're boring. I want to see strange animals. Fierce ones are the best. I hope there's one this year."

When they arrived in the village, a sale was just starting. Lots of horses were standing in a row, their owners holding their bridles whilst the auctioneer, a fat man wearing a gold chain round his neck, walked along the row followed by a crowd of men and women. He stopped by each horse and asked the owner to tell the crowd all about it. Then he examined it carefully and, in a loud voice, made comments about its age and condition.

They arrived in time to hear a man in a brown smock telling the auctioneer about his sad-looking horse.

"It's a good strong horse and it's in the best of health. It grieves me to have to sell it but I can't afford to feed it anymore."

There was some murmuring in the crowd.

Someone shouted, "How old is it?"

"Only three years." Laughter rippled through the crowd.

The auctioneer looked at the poor condition of the animal: its matted coat, its sagging back, its dim eyes and its worn teeth.

"Three years old? Thirty, more like it! It's a wonder it can manage to stand up." The crowd jeered and laughed.

The auctioneer turned to the crowd. "What am I offered for this fine animal?"

There were no bids.

The next two horses were also old and looked in poor condition. Again, nobody wanted to buy them.

The auctioneer moved to the next horse. This animal was young and healthy, and had a lovely glossy black coat. Caitlin immediately took a liking to it. She thought how wonderful it would be if she owned it and was able to ride it whenever she liked.

She said to her father, "Dad, I do like this horse. Will you buy it for me?"

Evan replied, "We already have an ox to do the ploughing and a donkey to carry things. We don't really need a horse. Anyway, horses are expensive."

She looked up at him trying to catch his eye. "Please Dad, buy it for me, please!"

Evan didn't have the heart to say no. "Well ... I suppose I could sell the donkey to help pay for it ... but I think it will be sold for more than I can afford."

"What am I bid?" shouted the auctioneer.

"A shilling," said a man with red hair.

Caitlin's father shouted, "Two shillings."

"Four shillings," countered red hair.

Evan hesitated and then shouted, "Six shillings."

There was a pause and it looked as though Evan had succeeded in buying the horse. Caitlin and Evan smiled at each other. Then ...

"Eight shillings," shouted a man wearing a green hat.

Evan whispered, "As I thought, it's too expensive for me."

Red hair bid again. "Ten shillings."

Green hat immediately said, "Eleven shillings."

Red hair made another bid. "Twelve shillings."

Green hat did not respond.

The auctioneer said, "Twelve shillings ... any advance on twelve shillings?"

There were no further bids.

"Sold to the gentleman with the red hair," shouted the auctioneer.

Caitlin was downcast; the horse would not be hers. Tears formed in her eyes and wet her cheeks. But Evan gave her hope.

"I know the man who bought the horse. His name is Alun. He farms the hillside just beyond the village." Evan went over to Alun and spoke to him.

Alun said to Caitlin, "Your father has told me how much you like the horse I've just bought. Any time you want to see it, just come to my farm. When it isn't doing any work I'll let you ride it, and afterwards you can help me groom it."

Caitlin felt a bit more cheerful and thanked Alun. To be able to go and see the horse and also ride it was the next best thing to actually owning it.

They left the row of horses and, a little further on, came across a man holding the bridle of a very strange animal. The man looked equally strange. He had a little pointed black beard, was dressed in long flowing white robes and wore a white head-dress with a black band fastened round it. The pale brown animal he held was bigger than a horse but, like a horse, it stood on four legs. There the resemblance ended. Its tail was thinner, its feet broader, its neck longer and its head was a completely different shape. So too was its back, which had a big hump on it.

Thomas approached its owner. "Why has this animal got a big hump? Did it break its back?"

Ali, the animal's owner, smiled. "No, it didn't. There's nothing wrong with its back. That's its proper shape. This animal is called a camel and it's perfectly healthy."

Thomas and Caitlin stood staring at the camel but were frightened to go too close in case it bit them. After all, it did have big teeth.

"Is it dangerous? Does it bite?" they asked.

"No, it's not dangerous," replied Ali, "but like horses, it will sometimes bite. I brought it here from the deserts of Barbary where people use them in place of horses."

Caitlin thought that very strange. "Why don't they use horses?"

"Well, there's no food or water in the desert and camels are able to go without either for many days."

"Why does it have a hump?" asked Thomas.

"The hump is full of fat. That's what it lives off while it's crossing the desert. If you like, you can both have a ride on it. I only charge a farthing."

Evan gave Ali a farthing and helped them onto the camel's back. With Ali leading the camel, they rode round the village green. Ali told them all about the deserts where camels usually live and also about other strange animals he had seen.

"One is like a donkey, but its coat is striped black and white. Another is huge and grey. It has four legs as thick as the trunks of big trees, a tiny little tail, small eyes, enormous ears, a very long nose and two tusks."

"That animal must be very fierce," said Thomas.

"No. The one I saw was as gentle as a kitten and I was even given a ride on its back."

"Where do you find all these strange animals?" asked Caitlin.

"Not in Britain nor in the land of the Romans, but in a far-off region called Africa."

Thomas said, "It must be exciting to live in Africa."

"Yes," said Ali, "but dangerous animals also live there, and some of them will kill and eat people."

Then he said, "The strangest animal I ever saw was a large red creature, a bit like a giant lizard. It had four scaly legs which ended in clawed feet, two large wings like those of a bat and a long tail with a thick pointed end. It looked very fierce. Unfortunately, I can't remember what it was called."

Thomas and Caitlin looked at one another. They knew instantly that he was talking about a dragon. They were excited.

"Where did you see this creature?" asked Thomas.

"I last saw it about a month ago at the horse market at Llanerch. Its owner said it could breathe fire but would not always oblige. I said I would give him a penny if he could make it do so. He tried hard to persuade it to breathe fire, even offering it a sack of its favourite food, but the animal just stood there looking miserable and refused. No animal I know can make fire and I don't really believe this one can."

"Where do you think it is now?" asked Caitlin.

"I don't know. But its owner said he's taking it to the Midsummer Fair at Aber next week."

Thomas asked, "Will you be going to Aber?"

"Yes."

"We'd like to see this animal. Can we come with you?"

"Only if your father or mother comes as well."

Thomas and Caitlin thanked Ali and left him.

When they were far enough away not to be heard, Caitlin said, "That dragon might be Russ's daughter Rosa. Remember Russ told us how Rosa was captured and sold to a travelling showman. Dragons live for hundreds of years, so it could be her. We must go to the Midsummer Fair and set her free."

"But how are we going to do that?" queried Thomas.

"Mum and Dad always go the Midsummer Fair. If we pester them they'll give in and take us with them. I don't know how we can rescue Rosa, but Emrys might have an idea."

Next day, they went to see Emrys. Caitlin repeated the story Ali had told them concerning a dragon in a cage and how Russ's daughter Rosa, had been captured long ago and sold to a showman. She also told him the dragon was going to be taken to the Midsummer Fair at Aber.

Thomas added, "We want to go to the Midsummer Fair. If it's Rosa, we'd like to rescue her."

"That won't be easy," said Emrys.

He cupped his chin in his hand, stared at the floor and looked thoughtful. Several seconds went by before he spoke.

"I have an idea. Let's talk about it." Soon they had made a plan.

Chapter 17

The Midsummer Fair

The Midsummer Fair was held in a big field on the edge of Aber. It was rather like the horse market only much bigger, but there were no horses or other animals for sale. Instead, there were traders selling the things people used in their daily lives. In those days villages had no shops, so it was only possible to buy many things by going into a town or attending a fair. Each year their parents went to the Midsummer Fair to buy bowls, cups, cloth and everything else they needed. Up until now, they had always left Thomas and Caitlin at home because they were thought to be too young to travel to Aber. However, now they were bigger, there was no longer a reason to leave them behind, which meant that Thomas and Caitlin didn't have much difficulty persuading their parents to agree to take them along.

Knowing they would find the journey arduous, Gwyn decided to test their resolve. "Aber's a long way off. It's seven miles over the mountains and we'll have to walk all the way there and all the way back. It'll be a slow and tiring journey because the tracks are rough, go up and down steep hills and cross several streams."

"Can't we ride on the donkey," asked Caitlin.

"No. We need the donkey to carry some brooms we are going to sell."

Thomas wasn't to be put off. "We're big now. I'm sure we'll be able to manage."

Their mother wasn't satisfied. "If it rains you'll get soaked to the skin, and if it's sunny you'll get roasted. It won't be any use complaining so you must be really sure you want to come with us".

Caitlin supported Thomas. "We definitely want to go to Aber, and we won't complain about anything."

"Are you sure?"

"Very sure," they both replied, being prepared to put up with anything in order to see the dragon in the cage.

Next day they got up even earlier than usual. Evan and Gwyn strapped two large baskets to the donkey, one on each side. In them they put two leather flasks filled with water and bundles of brooms they had made out of hazel twigs. They intended to sell the brooms at the fair and use the money to buy the things they needed.

As the sun rose, they walked down the track to the village and splashed through the ford. Passing the last of the village cottages and Alun's farm, they started to climb the hill. The path rose steeply making their legs ache and causing them to pant. Thomas and Caitlin had never been this way before and the trip soon began to seem like an adventure. Further up the hill, coarse grass gave way to thick bracken, almost as tall as Thomas, and the path became rougher. They had to avoid large stones sticking out of the ground. If Evan hadn't carefully led the donkey round them, these would have caused it to stumble.

The day was warm and the effort of walking uphill made them sweat. It was cloudy and the sun only occasionally broke through. This was fortunate, otherwise it would have been unbearably hot. After a few brief rest stops, they reached what they had thought would be the top of the hill. However, it wasn't; the real top only now came into view.

Dismayed at the prospect of another climb, Thomas grumbled, "I'm tired and thirsty. How much further is it?"

"I told you the journey would be long and tiring," said Gwyn, "and you promised not to complain. We haven't gone far yet. There are miles and miles still to go."

"Sorry," said Thomas sulkily. "I won't complain again."

"Well, I'm not complaining," said Caitlin haughtily.

"Sit on the rocks and rest," said Evan, "and have some water to drink."

While they rested they looked back along the path. The village lay far below. Its cottages looked tiny, the people like ants. In the distance they could see the whole of the forest. For the first time, they realised how big it was. They could also see the Afon Glas. Following it with their eyes they saw it join another bigger river ... just as their father had told them.

Suddenly, Thomas exclaimed, "I can see the sea!"

"Where, where?" asked Caitlin excitedly. "Show me."

Thomas pointed with his finger. Far away, on the horizon, almost lost in the heat haze, they could see a shimmering narrow yellow strip of sand and, above it, the grey-blue water of the sea.

"Is that where we are going? Is Aber by the sea?" asked Caitlin, her eyes sparkling with excitement.

"No," replied Gwyn. "Aber is the place where the Afon Glas joins the big river. It's miles from the sea."

The disappointment showed on Caitlin's face. "Oh, what a shame," she said.

They continued walking uphill until eventually they came to the edge of a plateau. The path ran across the plateau, weaving this way and that in order to avoid huge masses of rock. Bracken didn't grow up here. Where it wasn't bare, the ground was covered with purple-flowered heather and tough moorland grasses. Some goats were grazing on the grasses and eating the leaves of the few stunted trees and bushes that grew there. Now the journey became quite pleasant. Walking across the plateau required little effort ... and the air was cooler than lower down.

A familiar yelping sound captured their attention. They looked up. Caught in a beam of sunlight, they saw a golden eagle soaring on the air currents.

"Aquila?" whispered Caitlin. Thomas nodded.

Even as they watched, it slowly drifted away in the direction of Aber.

About a mile further on, the path skirted a particularly large mass of rock. As they neared it, a short, bearded muscular figure dressed in goat skins emerged from a cave. Holding a stout staff, he stood on top of the rock, brushed his straggly shoulder-length hair from his face, shielded his eyes from the sun and greeted them.

"Good morning. Where are you all going this fine day?"

"We're off to the Midsummer Fair," replied Evan.

"I thought so. You are the third party to pass this way today. Do you know the path?"

"Of course. We've been to Aber many times and know the path well."

"But when did you last go?"

"Last year."

"Well, the route is different now," said the goatherd. "Part of the path near the river was swept away in last winter's floods. If you pay me a farthing, I'll guide you and show you the new path."

They debated whether they should pay the goatherd, or try to find the way themselves. In the end, they decided to pay him.

"My name is Idris. During the summer I live up here while my goats feed on the mountain top. Each autumn I take them down to my farm near Aber to spend the winter there. When I came up here in the spring, I had to find a new path. That's why I know the way."

They followed Idris across the plateau for about a mile, going in a direction unfamiliar to Evan and

Gwyn. Then they climbed up onto a rocky ridge and walked along it for a considerable distance before it came to an end. There, Idris left them.

"If you follow this path it'll take you to Aber. Goodbye. Have a safe journey."

At about midday they arrived at Aber. Built on a triangle of high ground where the two rivers met, it was a much bigger place than Caerdraig. Entering the main street, Evan asked a passer-by where the fair was being held. The man pointed.

"It's in a big field on the edge of the town, close to that wooded hill."

"Is it in the usual place?" Thomas asked his father.

"Yes. It's been held there for years now."

Thomas was relieved. If it had been in a different place, it would have ruined their plans for rescuing Rosa.

In the field were rows and rows of stalls displaying all sorts of goods. Behind the stalls were the vendors, all shouting loudly to attract the attention of passers-by. Evan and his family walked along the rows until they found an empty stall. Gwyn tethered the donkey and started to unload the brooms.

"Thomas, Caitlin, come and help," she said.

When the brooms had all been displayed, Evan joined in the shouting.

"New brooms for sale. Only a farthing each. Finer ones you won't find anywhere. Only a farthing each!"

Passers-by stopped to look. Some examined the brooms and, satisfied they were strongly made, bought them. After about an hour, all had been sold. They now had an extra ten silver pennies to spend.

While their parents were selling brooms, Thomas and Caitlin searched for the dragon. They scoured the field but couldn't find it. On the way back to their parents' stall they met Ali with his camel.

"Hello," said Ali. "I see you managed to persuade your parents to bring you here."

"Yes," replied Thomas. "We just had to see the big red beast you told us about, but we haven't been able to find it. Is it here?"

"No, I don't think so. I haven't seen it anywhere. But Rolf, who owns it, told me he would definitely be coming here."

"Oh, I do hope he comes," said Caitlin.

They were disappointed the dragon hadn't arrived and began to think Rolf wasn't coming. With glum faces they wandered off and rejoined their parents, who were now looking for the things they had come to buy. Their mother paused to buy a big earthenware bowl. She needed it for baking bread because the one she had bought last year had a crack in it. Further on, their father bought a small scythe for cutting hay or corn. This was for Thomas to use. Then they heard a strange noise. Nearby was a man selling wooden rattles.

"Caitlin, they look fun. I'd like one of those, wouldn't you?" said Thomas.

"Dad, buy us a rattle."

"Those rattles aren't toys," replied Evan. "They're used to scare away the sparrows that come to eat the ripening corn. I'll buy you one each. You can play with them as much as you like, provided you take it in turns to frighten the sparrows."

Swinging the rattles and feeling brighter they continued wandering round the fair.

Soon their noses twitched as they smelt the delicious odour of roast pork wafting through the air. Not having eaten since leaving home, it made them feel hungry. Following the odour, they came to a tent, outside which a charcoal fire burned. A large red-faced man wearing a white apron was turning a spit on which was skewered a small pig. The flames licked the pork and fat dripped from it into the fire, making sizzling noises and producing bright little flames.

"How much do you want for a slice of pork?" asked Evan.

"Together with a big piece of bread, only a farthing," said the man.

"Give me four pieces please."

The man cut four slices of pork, each as thick as a man's thumb, and four equally thick slices of bread.

"That'll be a penny."

Evan handed him a silver penny. They sat down on the grass and ate.

Chapter 18

Rosa Rescued

They had just finished eating when a commotion on the far side of the field attracted their attention. People were shouting excitedly and running.

"Look at that!" shouted one man. "Have you ever seen anything like it?"

He hurried on.

Thomas and Caitlin followed him to where a large crowd had gathered but could not see over people's heads.

"Caitlin, follow me," said Thomas, as he pushed his way through the crowd's legs.

Reaching the front, they saw it. Coming into the field, pulled by six huge cart horses, was an enormous cage and in it was a dragon, only part of which could be seen. It was the first time a dragon had been taken to the Midsummer Fair and hardly anybody present had seen one before. How big it

179

was and how fierce it looked! People were a bit frightened by it, but still surged forward for a closer look.

When he had parked the cage, Rolf led the horses away to be fed and watered while his assistant Edwin put up screens to block the view of the dragon.

On returning, Rolf climbed up, stood in front of the cage and shouted, "Come and see the dragon. For only half a penny you can have a proper look at the rarest animal in the world."

"Ooh!" went the crowd.

They thought half a penny was too much to pay simply to have a look at an animal, no matter how rare, and grumbled among themselves about the cost.

Annoyed, the showman shouted, "Come on, come on. It's not a lot of money. How much do you think it costs to feed six horses and a beast as big as this? You might never get the chance to see a dragon again ... and one that can breathe fire!"

The crowd muttered but, being curious about its supposed ability to breathe fire, started to go forward.

"Can it really breathe fire?" one man asked.

"Yes," said Rolf. "She really can breathe fire ... usually when she's angry."

At first, just a few people paid to have a closer look, but then more and more paid the halfpenny and went inside the enclosure.

To encourage them Rolf shouted, "If enough of you pay, I'll try to get her to breathe fire."

Very soon, most of the people in the field had paid to look at the dragon and were standing around waiting to see it breathe fire.

Growing impatient, people began to shout, "When is it going to breathe fire? Let's see it breathe fire!"

"Breathe fire, breathe fire, breathe fire ..." they chanted in unison.

Rolf went up to the dragon, spoke to her and offered her some food, but she refused to eat. Turning her back on the crowd, she lay down on the floor of the cage. The crowd booed loudly. Believing Rolf was telling lies, they gradually dispersed.

Later, when it quietened down and only an occasional person came to see the dragon, Rolf and Edwin went off to have something to eat and drink, leaving the dragon unattended. Thomas and Caitlin seized their chance. They went up to the cage and spoke to the dragon.

"Are you Russ's daughter?" asked Thomas.

The dragon raised her head and stared, but did not reply. She obviously didn't trust them. They wondered what to do. Caitlin fingered the pendant she wore round her neck. Emrys had made it using Blue Fish's pearl and some silver he extracted from the crystals they found underground. She drew it out from under her tunic and showed it to the dragon. The dragon stared at the pearl. Then she spoke.

Their heads tingled as they heard her say, "Who are you? Why have you got one of Blue Fish's pearls?"

Caitlin said, "We haven't time to explain. You'll have to trust us. Are you Rosa?"

"Yes," replied the dragon. "I am Rosa. Long, long ago, I was captured by the Earl's men and sold to a showman. As each showman got too old to travel around, he sold me to another." She began to weep. "I think I'll be a prisoner until the day I die."

Thomas said, "Don't cry. We've come to rescue you. Soon you won't be a prisoner anymore."

He looked around. "Rolf will soon be back so we must act quickly. Can you fly?"

"Yes. But not very strongly. Rolf only occasionally allows me to fly, and then it's always on the end of a very strong chain."

"D'you see the wood on the hill over there? D'you think you could fly as far as that?"

"I think so."

"Good," said Thomas. "When we let you out, fly over the wood until you see a big barn in a clearing. Standing next to it will be an old man. He'll be waiting for you and will hide you in the barn until it's safe to take you back to the forest."

While Caitlin kept watch, Thomas pulled back the heavy iron bolts securing the huge door. He didn't have the strength to open the door but Rosa helped by leaning against it. The dragon climbed onto the ground, trampled down the screens and flexed her wings. For take-off she needed a clear stretch of ground, but there were lots of people standing around and more and more were coming to see what was happening. To clear the way, she breathed fire. With a loud roar, a huge flame rolled across the ground in front of her. Everyone scattered, leaving the ground clear. Beating her wings, she ran forward. Harder and harder she beat them. People watched in amazement as the dragon slowly took to the air. She struggled to gain height and it was only with the greatest effort she managed to clear the tops of the trees. Even then, her tail brushed against the upper branches scattering twigs and leaves everywhere.

Rolf and Edwin heard the noise and saw Rosa take off. They came running and shouting but it was too late, she had gone. All they could see was a small winged figure flying just above the trees of the wood. Quite suddenly she disappeared from view as she dropped down among the trees.

Running to the wood, they started looking for Rosa. During the search they came across the clearing in which was situated the old barn. Sat on a heap of logs outside the barn was a tall, thin old man holding a woodcutter's axe.

"Woodcutter," said Rolf, "I'm a showman and I take a dragon round the country to show at fairs. I was showing it at the Midsummer Fair when it escaped. I think it's hiding somewhere in this wood. Have you seen it?"

With a smile on his face, the old man looked at Rolf and said, "A showman, you say. Then you'll be wanting a bear cub. Showmen always have dancing bears. I know where there's a bear with cubs. If you give me a gold piece, I'll take you there."

"No, no," snapped Rolf, "not a bear cub, a dragon!"

The old man grinned foolishly, "A dragon, what's that?"

"It's a big fierce-looking creature with leathery wings."

"Oh, I know what you mean. Follow me," said the old man.

He led Rolf and Edwin on a long, winding journey. They walked through tall nettles which stung their legs, through thorn bushes which tore their clothes, and through a large patch of brambles which scratched their hands and faces. Strangely, the old man was unaffected but Rolf and his companion didn't notice that. The journey went on and on.

After a while, sounding cross, Rolf said to the old man, "I'm sure we passed this big oak tree before. Are you sure you know where you are going?"

"Yes," replied the old man. "I saw the creature with leathery wings only an hour ago. It was over there."

He pointed in the direction of a large hollow tree some distance away, on the other side of a swamp. Up to their waists in dirty water and stinking black mud, they struggled through the swamp and finally arrived at the hollow tree.

"Where is it?" demanded Rolf. "I can't see it anywhere."

The old man pointed to the tree. "It's in there," he declared triumphantly.

"It can't be!" shouted Rolf. "A dragon is much too big to fit inside a tree."

"But it is," said the old man as he banged on the tree. Out flew a large bat.

"See, it's got leathery wings, just like you said."

Rolf was now very angry and his face turned bright red with rage.

"You silly old fool," he bellowed. "I'm scratched, nettled and covered in mud and all for nothing!" ... and off he and his assistant stalked.

As he watched them disappear among the trees, the old man fingered the gold coin Rolf had given him. When they were completely out of sight, he stood and laughed and laughed... until tears ran down his cheeks.

A few days later, after the Midsummer Fair ended, Emrys brought Rosa back to the forest where she was reunited with Russ and his family. For months afterwards, she amused the other dragons by telling them stories about the different showmen who had owned her, the places to which she had been taken and the events that had occurred, some funny, some sad and some dangerous.

The End